MEET THE FORTUNES

Fortune of the Month: Charles Fortune Chesterfield

Age: 29

Vital statistics: Dark, sexy hair women love to tousle, seductive blue eyes. Six feet plus of honest-to-goodness princely charisma.

Claim to fame: "Bonnie Lord Charlie" is an international hottie whose TV commercials for British tourism promise visitors to England "the royal treatment."

Romantic prospects: Are you kidding?

"Social media would have me as some kind of lothario. This is not strictly true. I do enjoy feminine attention. I can't help it if women find me irresistible. I do not fear commitment; I simply choose to avoid it.

But now there's Alice. And Flynn. My son! From the moment I found out he was mine, everything changed. I've promised to do everything in my power to be a good father to my boy, and that means keeping my hands off Flynn's mom. Strictly friends, she says. It's what she wants. It's the right thing to do. And I'm bloody certain it's going to kill me."

**THE FORTUNES OF TEXAS:
ALL FORTUNE'S CHILDREN—
Money. Family. Cowboys.
Meet the Austin Fortunes!**

Dear Reader,

As young girls, many of us dreamed of one day finding our own Prince Charming. Charles Fortune Chesterfield may not be royalty, but he's handsome, smart, flirty and he loves women. Plus, there's that yummy British accent. In fact, he's become the poster boy for British tourism, and women around the world visit England hoping to receive "the royal treatment" from Charles.

But during a trip to visit his family in Texas, Charles receives a call from a woman he knew for only one unforgettable weekend. It's a call that will change his life in ways he never expected.

When Alice Meyers introduces Charles to his baby son, she isn't sure how the famous playboy will react. In her wildest dreams, she never imagined that Charles would embrace the role of father. And his bond with their baby soon leads to a connection between Charles and Alice that neither can deny. But can two people from opposite worlds overcome their differences to find true love?

I hope you enjoy Charles and Alice's story because I had a great time writing it! I'd love to hear from you at michellemajor.com or through Facebook (Facebook.com/michellemajorbooks) or Twitter (@michelle_major1).

All the best,

Michelle Major

Fortune's Special Delivery

Michelle Major

HARLEQUIN® SPECIAL EDITION®

Special thanks and acknowledgment to Michelle Major
for her contribution to the
Fortunes of Texas: All Fortune's Children continuity.

ISBN-13: 978-0-373-65949-4

Fortune's Special Delivery

Copyright © 2016 by Harlequin Books S.A.

PLEASE RECYCLE
THIS PRODUCT IS RECYCLABLE

Recycling programs
for this product may
not exist in your area.

This edition published by arrangement with Harlequin Books S.A.

For questions and comments about the quality of this book, please contact us at CustomerService@Harlequin.com.

Printed in U.S.A.

www.Harlequin.com

Michelle Major grew up in Ohio but dreamed of living in the mountains. Soon after graduating with a degree in journalism, she pointed her car west and settled in Colorado. Her life and house are filled with one great husband, two beautiful kids, a few furry pets and several well-behaved reptiles. She's grateful to have found her passion writing stories with happy endings. Michelle loves to hear from her readers at michellemajor.com.

Books by Michelle Major

Harlequin Special Edition

Crimson, Colorado

A Baby and a Betrothal
A Very Crimson Christmas
Suddenly a Father
A Second Chance on Crimson Ranch
A Kiss on Crimson Ranch

A Brevia Beginning
Her Accidental Engagement
Still the One

The Fortunes of Texas: Cowboy Country

The Taming of Delaney Fortune

Visit the Author Profile page at Harlequin.com for more titles.

To all the Fortunes readers. I'm thrilled to be celebrating the 20th anniversary with you!

Chapter One

"A toast to your marriage."

Charles Fortune Chesterfield lifted his glass of deep red cabernet, unable to hide the smile that curved one corner of his mouth. "Or should I call it your unmarriage? Your remarriage?" He winked at his sister Lucie, sitting across the table from him in the trendy Austin restaurant. It was early April and the weather in Central Texas was quite fine, a welcome change from the dreary rain of a London spring. He would rather have been sitting at a table on the restaurant's spacious patio, enjoying the fresh air and the sound of the city passing by them. Unfortunately, the paparazzi hounded his family wherever they went, so Charles and Lucie were huddled in a quiet booth in the back of the restaurant.

"Don't be cheeky, Charles," Lucie answered in a clipped tone, her hazel eyes flashing. "If you came all the way to Texas to tease me, you should have stayed in London."

"I'm happy for you, Luce." Charles set down his wineglass and grabbed his younger sister's hand, giving it a squeeze. "Truly I am. That's why Austin was my first stop on this trip."

"And…" she prompted, her smile returning.

"You and Chase make a lovely couple," he offered. "It's obvious how much he loves you." Charles hoped his sister realized he was sincere. He hadn't seen her as happy as she was now, reunited with her first love and husband, Texas oilman Chase Parker. Few had known about Lucie's impulsive wedding when she was only seventeen until the fact that she and Chase were still married came to light last month. Charles had hated watching his younger sister hounded by the press, but true love had triumphed in the end.

He'd flown in yesterday from London and gone straight to dinner with Chase and Lucie at the sprawling Parker ranch outside town. Even jet-lagged, he'd been able to see how much they loved each other. His family had wasted no time in filling him in on the news from Horseback Hollow, the small Texas town the rest of his siblings called home. Lucie had also informed him that family matriarch and cosmetics mogul Kate Fortune was still in Austin and apparently meeting with their generation of Fortune children to look for someone to take over the empire built on her Fortune Youth Serum.

"Chase is perfect," Lucie agreed now, "although I wouldn't recommend calling him 'lovely' to his face. A native Texan won't appreciate that description, Charles. But I'm talking about you." She punched a few keys on her cell phone and lifted it for a better view. She'd gone to one of the online tabloid sites so popular in Britain.

The headline displayed on the small screen read Is the Third Time a Charm for Bonnie Lord Charlie? An obvious reference to Charles's two previous broken engagements. Below the headline was a grainy photo of Charles and a beautiful, thin and very regal-looking brunette.

"Lady Caterina Hayworth?" Lucie asked, her brow puckered. "Tell me you're not engaged to Conniving Cat. I know you like your women brainless and beautiful, but she's a social climber of the worst sort. You must know she wants your celebrity status as much as she wants you."

"I hate that nickname," he muttered, running his finger along the smooth screen as if he could blot out the maddening words.

"Conniving Cat?" Lucie waved a hand in the air. "Perhaps it isn't kind, but you must admit—"

"Not that one," he clarified. "Hell, Caterina loves the moniker. I think she was the one to start it. I mean 'Bonnie Lord Charlie.'" He scrubbed a hand over his face, the transatlantic time change suddenly catching up with him tenfold. "Jensen is the one with the title." Their mother, Josephine May Fortune Chesterfield, had married Sir Simon Chesterfield after ending her first, loveless marriage to Rhys Henry Hayes. "The press doesn't feel the need to give Brodie or Oliver a fake title," Charles said, referring to their two older half brothers from Josephine's first marriage. "And calling me 'bonnie' is ridiculous. I'm a twenty-nine-year-old man, not a wee lad toddling around in rompers."

"You *are* quite handsome." Lucie's smile turned sympathetic. "I'm sure it's meant as a compliment."

"It's an implied dig that I don't *do* anything, that I have nothing to offer but my face and my family's good name. No use denying it."

Her slim shoulders stiffened. "You do plenty, Charles. I think your ads single-handedly doubled the number of women vacationing in Britain over the past year."

He fought back a grimace, even though he had no one but himself to blame. The ad campaign that featured him promising visitors to England "the royal treatment" had started as a joke during a meeting he'd attended with the British Tourism Council two years ago. He'd been expected to bring ideas to the table, but had spent the night before the meeting clubbing with friends and had shown up to the meeting a half hour late with a raging headache. He'd pitched the Royal Treatment campaign as a jest, but the council had loved it. Before he knew what was happening, Charles ended up the star of a series of print and television ads, wearing a tux in front of various British monuments, giving it his best James Bond–meets–Mr. Darcy impression.

He was happy to do his part for queen and country, but lately wished his contribution could be of a more meaningful sort. Lucie, like their mother, devoted herself to various charitable organizations. Their brother Jensen was a successful financier. Everyone in his family had something of substance to offer.

Except Charles.

That, too, was his fault. For years he'd cultivated his image as a good-time guy. He'd been the charmer in his family as a kid, perpetually entertaining his parents and siblings, always good for a laugh. After Sir Simon died, it had seemed the right thing to do to make his mother smile as often as he could. So that's what people had come to expect from him—a good time. Only his father had ever seemed to want him to be something more.

"That is part of why I'm here. I have meetings set up with the Texas Tourism Board next week. We'd like to do some cross-promotions—Texans and high tea. That sort of thing." He leaned forward. "Did you know almost three million Americans are projected to visit England this year?"

"And most of them want 'the royal treatment'?" Lucie asked with a laugh.

Charles forced a smile. He had a reputation to uphold, after all. "I suppose. You're right about me needing an escape. There's work and family, but I also needed to get away from the press. Cat and I were nowhere near to being engaged. We weren't even a proper couple."

Lucie taped a finger on the cell phone screen. "Did she know that?"

"Chalk it up to selective hearing on her part," Charles said. "Don't get me wrong, she's a lovely lady." He sighed. "They're all lovely ladies."

"But what about the right woman, Charles?" Lucie took a sip of her wine and waved away the waiter who approached their table. "Now that Chase and I are together, you're officially the last man standing in the family. Brodie, Oliver, Jensen and Amelia are happy in Horseback Hollow. Even Mum seems to have found love again."

"Jensen mentioned a burgeoning romance with Orlando Mendoza." Charles was happy for his mother, although it was difficult to imagine her with anyone but his father.

"She's glowing," Lucie said with a wistful sigh.

"Then the two of you have that in common, dear sister." Charles twirled the stem of the wineglass between two fingers. "Marriage...remarriage...whatever you want to call it agrees with you. But I don't believe there's only one woman in the world for me."

"Because you haven't met her yet," Lucie argued.

"I've met plenty of women."

"And bedded most of them."

Charles took a long drink of wine. "I'm absolutely *not* having this conversation with my sister."

"If you'd only—"

At that moment, Charles's cell phone rang. He drew the device out of his coat pocket as Lucie frowned.

"Send the call to voice mail," she told him with her best sisterly glare. "I'm not finished lecturing you."

He grinned, then glanced at the display. "Sorry, sis, it's an Austin number. Might be important *royal* business." But when he accepted the call and said hello, whoever was on the other end of the line was silent. "Anyone there?" he asked into the phone.

He was about to hang up when he heard a funny squeak that might have been "hello."

A throat cleared. "Is this Charles?" a woman's voice asked.

"Who wants to know?" he responded, then met Lucie's curious gaze and shrugged his shoulders.

"Hang up," his sister whispered.

Charles understood her reaction. The caller was likely a reporter trying to track him down, or one of the frequent fame hounds who'd come after his family through the years, especially since their connection to the prominent Fortunes was revealed. Charles, like all the Fortune Chesterfields, had learned to guard his privacy—one more reason the tabloid photo with Lady Caterina irked him.

But something about the way the woman on the other

end of the phone spoke his name intrigued him. Her voice was soft, with a sweet Texas drawl and more than a hint of nerves. Charles might be a magnet for women, but the timid girls typically gave him a wide berth.

"This is Alice," the woman told him.

"Alice," he repeated, liking the way the two syllables sounded on his tongue. But he had no recognition of an Alice from his past.

"Alice Meyers," she continued, a little breathlessly. "I'm sorry to call you out of the blue. I got your number from the tourism board office."

Right. Suddenly an image—a beautiful blonde, with long legs and a shy but sexy smile—popped into his mind.

Alice cleared her throat again. "We met last year—"

"At the tourism conference here in Austin," he continued. "I remember you." Charles tried to hide his small smile from Lucie. What he remembered most about Alice was spending a blissful night with her in his hotel room after the conference ended. He'd even asked for her number, something he rarely did after a casual dalliance. But he'd liked Alice Meyers, and he'd thought she liked him. Too bad when he'd come out of the shower the next morning she'd disappeared from his hotel room and his life.

Now, more than a year later, she was ringing him. Charles felt his smile widen. Intriguing, indeed.

Alice breathed a sigh of relief that Charles remembered her. Of course, she'd known who he was before they'd met at the bar in the conference hotel last spring. Every woman between the ages of ten and ninety knew

Bonnie Lord Charlie. But she hadn't expected him to commit her to memory. Men rarely did.

She'd followed his romantic exploits in the tabloids since their encounter, and it was a wonder Charles could remember what girl he was with on any given night. The man seemed to be the British equivalent of the Energizer Bunny when it came to women.

"Alice, are you still there?" His crisp accent broke through her musings.

"I need to see you," she blurted, then bit down hard on her lip as silence greeted her outburst. He was bound to think she was a stalker for calling him out of blue and making such a bold request.

"That's a lovely offer," he said finally, sounding every bit the aristocrat he was. How was it possible for him to sound more British than before? "But I'm fairly booked on this visit."

"It's important," she whispered, swallowing back the emotion clogging her throat. "I promise I won't take much of your time."

"Can you give me a hint what this mysterious meeting might entail?"

"It's personal and…" She paused, then added, "Please, Charles."

There was another long moment of silence. Alice checked her phone to make sure Charles hadn't hung up on her. She wouldn't exactly blame him. He was handsome, rich, and famous around the world. She was nobody, yet was demanding precious time from him. But even if he said no now, Alice couldn't give up. Seeing Charles again was too important.

"Tomorrow morning," he said suddenly.

"Gr-great," she stammered, shocked that he'd agreed.

The fingers holding the phone trembled with both nerves and exhilaration. "We could meet in Zilker Park. Are you familiar with it?"

"I am."

"There's a bench under a big oak tree near the entrance of the Zilker Botanical Garden. How about ten o'clock?"

"Very good. I'll see you in the morning, Alice."

The way he spoke her name made sparks zing low in her belly. His accent made every word sound like a caress. She shook her head, needing to keep her wits about her. As good a time as she'd had with Charles, she hadn't contacted him for her sake. "Goodbye, Charles. Thank you."

As the call ended, she pulled the phone away from her head, her hand trembling as she stared at it. "I did it," she whispered, glancing at the baby sleeping in the swing in the corner of the room. Her son, Flynn, was a champion napper at four months, which was one of the few things that had made being a single mom a tiny bit easier for Alice.

"Come here and tell me everything." She turned to see her best friend, Meredith Doan, gesturing wildly from the galley kitchen in Alice's two-bedroom apartment. Meredith was the only person who knew about Charles, and Alice had confided in her friend only recently, needing an ally to bolster her confidence.

"It went well," Alice said quietly as she stepped into the small space. "We're meeting tomorrow morning."

"You look like you need this," Meredith said, handing Alice a glass of white wine. "Your face is beet red. Charles remembered you?"

"Yes, after a moment." Alice took a deep breath, her first since dialing Charles's number.

"Tell me again how you ended up having an affair with Bonnie Lord Charlie."

"It wasn't exactly an affair," Alice answered, taking a fortifying sip of wine. "It was one night. We met at the annual Texas tourism conference last spring. There was an international focus, so the board invited representatives from several European countries to attend. Charles has ties in Texas now through the Fortunes, so he came from Britain."

Meredith wiggled her eyebrows. "And you snagged yourself a royal? Nice work, Meyers. I didn't think you had it in you."

"I didn't," Alice said quickly. "I don't. It wasn't like that, Meredith. It was special."

"They all are, sweetie."

Alice knew she would have a difficult time convincing her friend. She'd met Meredith her first day working at the Texas Tourism Board, and they'd struck up an unlikely friendship. Meredith worked in the marketing department and was as outgoing off the clock as she was on the job. Since Alice had known her, Meredith had dated a number of guys and even had a few random hookups. Alice, on the other hand, had no one.

Until Charles.

When they'd met at an industry reception the last night of the conference, Alice had expected him to look right past her. Almost everyone did, so she was used to it. There'd been a flurry of Texas women vying for his attention, flirting like they did it for a living. Alice had barely been able to make eye contact when she and Charles had been introduced. He was so handsome, several inches taller than her own five foot nine. His dark hair was expensively cut but perpetually tousled from his habit of running his fingers through it. His brilliant blue eyes seemed to see right into her soul.

It had been a silly thought, and she'd spent the rest of the party watching him laugh and joke with the crowd that constantly surrounded him. He was like a fun magnet and almost exactly her opposite in every way. As the dancing started midway through the evening, with conference attendees from all different countries and backgrounds letting loose in the hotel bar, Alice had been ready to leave. Before she could, Charles had slipped into the booth next to her. He'd told her he'd been watching her all night, waiting for a moment alone with her.

It had been difficult to believe, but he'd stayed at her side the rest of the evening. They'd talked about everything and nothing, and to her surprise, Charles had seemed as happy to escape the noise and bustle of the crowd as Alice. So when he'd invited her up to his room…

"What happened to the condom?" Meredith said, pointing a finger at her. "Your first time out of the gate and you don't use protection? I thought I'd taught you better."

"We did use protection," Alice protested weakly. "I got pregnant anyway. They aren't one hundred percent effective. And I guess saving the condom for a couple years wasn't such a great idea, after all."

After one too many cosmos at a happy hour shortly after she'd met Meredith, Alice had lamented her perennial virginity to her new friend. Alice hadn't set out to still be a virgin at age twenty-five, but she'd been shy and awkward through her teen years and focused on her classes during college. She'd expected to meet Mr. Right at some point, but when he never materialized, decided she might have to settle for Mr. Right Now. She'd hoped gregarious Meredith could help her, and the first thing her new friend had done was give Alice a condom to keep in her wallet.

It had stayed there for two years, until the night with Charles. Of course, he'd had protection, but she'd insisted on using hers. It meant something to her, a rite of passage of sorts. Even though it had been only one night—well, twice in one night—when she'd left his hotel the next morning, her purse had felt ten pounds lighter on her shoulder.

Only six weeks later, when she couldn't keep down her breakfast each morning, did she realize how foolish she'd truly been.

"You know this means Flynn is a Fortune," Meredith said in an awestruck tone.

Alice set her wineglass on the quartz counter, her fingers suddenly unsteady again. "He's my baby, Mer. Mine." Flynn was everything to her.

"But you're going to tell Charles."

"He deserves to know." She crossed her arms over her chest, the implications of what she'd put into motion settling like a west Texas dust storm on her shoulders. "I doubt he'll even want to be involved. Everyone knows his reputation. I'm sure tomorrow will be the last time Flynn and I will ever see Charles."

Chapter Two

The next morning was bright and warm, the exact weather Charles was coming to expect from Austin in April. He'd booked a room at the Four Seasons Hotel for the duration of his visit, even though Lucie had invited him to stay at the Parker ranch outside town. But Charles liked the vibe of downtown Austin, and despite his social nature, he also appreciated time alone. Later, the day would turn hot and humid, but it was pleasant enough now that he'd chosen to walk the few miles from his hotel, situated on Lady Bird Lake, the reservoir in downtown Austin, over to Zilker Park.

The walkway was busy, and he enjoyed watching men and women running, mothers with small children and strollers, and the trees and flowers that lined the path. Even more, he enjoyed the anonymity. A few people did a double take when he passed, but no one stopped him.

In London, he could barely get from his flat to the corner coffee shop without a camera flashing. This was a welcome change.

By the time he spotted the striking blonde sitting on the park bench outside the Zilker Botanical Garden entrance, Charles felt more relaxed than he had in ages.

Alice Meyers.

Yes, he remembered her. She was typing something into her phone, so he had a minute to study her. She was as lovely as she'd been a year ago and perhaps a bit curvier. The change suited her. Her pale hair was pulled back into a loose bun, a few strands escaping to brush across her cheek. Her skin was smooth and pale in contrast to her lush mouth. He'd kissed those lips all night long, never tiring of the taste of her.

Charles ran a hand through his hair, surprised at the sudden rush of memories. He didn't know why Alice had contacted him after so long, and there were plenty of women who meant more to him than she did. He approached slowly, waiting for her to glance up. She wore a silk blouse in a soft pink hue, tailored jeans and the most delectable pair of intricately strappy sandals he'd ever seen. The heels she'd worn the night they met had been just as unique, and he was irrationally glad that amazing shoes seemed to be a staple for her.

He was almost in front of her when she finally looked away from her phone. Her big hazel eyes widened and color tinged her cheeks.

"Charles," she breathed, quickly standing and thrusting a hand toward him.

He had every intention of shaking her hand, but at the last minute grasped her fingers and lifted her hand to his mouth, brushing his lips across her knuckles.

He forced himself to release her hand, and took a step back.

"Good morning, Alice."

"Hello," she said. "Thank you for meeting me." The pulse in her delicate neck fluttered wildly, and she swallowed. For some reason, her agitation made him relax. Certainly someone so nervous wouldn't be preparing to blackmail him.

"I'm glad you called," he said, making his tone reassuring. Whatever her reason for wanting to see him, Alice clearly needed some encouragement right now. Charles didn't consider himself the nurturing type but this woman seemed to bring something new to the surface in him.

"You are?" She sounded dubious, and it was hard to tell whom she doubted more—herself or him.

"I am." He flashed his most charming smile. "I enjoyed our time together last year, brief as the encounter turned out to be. If you—"

A sharp cry interrupted him. Alice turned to the buggy next to the park bench. He'd been so intent on her as he approached, he hadn't noticed it before. The stroller was one of those fancy American types, not the traditional pram many mums in Britain favored. This one was dark gray with navy blue trim and seemed as sturdy as a tank with an infant seat snapped into the top. Alice pushed back the cover to reveal a small baby peering out at them.

"This is my son," she said quickly. "His binky fell out." She reached under the baby and pulled out a piece of green rubber, popping it deftly in the boy's mouth just as he opened it to cry again. He began sucking and within seconds took a deep breath and seemed to settle back to watch the morning go by from his baby stroller throne.

"A real little prince you have there," Charles said, taking a step closer to the stroller.

Alice blinked at him as if he'd just said her son was next in line to the British throne.

"Figure of speech," he clarified. "How old is the lad?"

"Four months," she whispered. "He's…he's everything to me."

"I can see why." Charles hadn't spent much time around babies until his siblings had started with their own progeny. He'd discovered he liked wee ones, assuming he could give them back to their parents when a nappy needed changing. He leaned over the stroller and the baby looked up at him, with blue eyes bright and clear like his nephew Ollie had at that age.

Charles felt a vise wrap around his chest. He stared at the dark-haired boy a few more seconds, then staggered back a step, clutching at his shirtfront. "That baby looks exactly like the boys in my family." He met Alice's gaze. "He looks like *me*."

She stared at him, a mix of emotions ranging from apprehension to relief flashing across her delicate features. One hand was wrapped around the stroller's handle, like a gust of wind was coming and she needed the buggy to ground her. "Yes," she said simply, after an awkward moment. "He's yours."

A dull roar filled Charles's head. He had a baby. A son. He was a father. It seemed impossible. Yes, he'd dated plenty of women, but he'd been careful. Always. He'd always…

"How did this happen?"

The baby made another noise, and Alice picked him

up, cradling the boy in her arms. "The usual way, I guess," she said with an almost apologetic smile. "That night at the conference—"

"I remember the bloody night," Charles yelled, then scrubbed a hand over his jaw as Alice flinched. He took a breath, made his voice lower. "But we used protection. As I remember, the first condom was yours."

As Alice nodded, her cheeks flamed bright pink. She lowered herself to the park bench, still holding the baby tight to her chest. "I'd been saving it," she told him. "For my...first time. That was a mistake."

For an instant, Charles wondered if she was referring to the old condom or choosing him to take her virginity. It had been obvious that she was inexperienced, but he hadn't realized the full extent of her innocence until he'd pushed inside her. He'd tried to be gentle, to make it good for her, but his desire and need for her had been a force like nothing he'd experienced before.

Misinterpreting his silence, she continued, "I didn't mean for it to happen. You have to believe me, Charles. If you want a DNA test, I understand."

He looked at Flynn and simply *knew* deep in his soul. This was his son. He might be shocked, but there was no doubt she was telling the truth. "No test," he told her curtly.

"It's never been my intention to trap you. I just thought you should know."

"Why now?" He paced back and forth in front of the bench, too frantic with conflicting emotions to stand still. "I should have bloody well known a year ago."

"What would you have done?"

He stopped to consider the question and turned to

Alice, who seemed to read his thoughts before even he knew them.

Her chin tipped up and her shoulders straightened. "I know who you are, Charles. I know how you live." Gone suddenly was the nervous, shy girl he'd encountered, and in her place was a fierce, formidable mother. She adjusted the infant in her arms and leaned forward. "I loved this baby from the moment I discovered I was pregnant. I was going to be his mother, no matter what anyone else thought of the decision."

Resolve mixed with tension in her gaze. Charles caught a brief glimpse of what a woman like Alice must have endured, making the choice to become a single mother. Who had supported her during the pregnancy and the baby's birth? Would he have stepped into that role if she *had* told him?

"I didn't say I don't want him," he said, the anger at not knowing disappearing as quickly as it had arrived. He sank next to her on the bench and lifted one finger to trace the top of the baby's small head. The boy had a decent amount of hair for a little one, dark and downy soft.

"You certainly didn't say you *did*," Alice countered.

Charles nodded, willing to acknowledge that, even if it wasn't the whole truth. "I'll admit this is quite a shock. I don't know you well, Alice, but I'd gather a one-night stand with a stranger isn't the way you planned to bring a child into the world."

She let out a small, tired laugh. "Nothing about this was part of my plan, but he's here now. I wouldn't change a thing."

"Does he have a name?"

Alice smiled. "Flynn. His name is Flynn Davis Meyers."

"A strong name," Charles told her. "I like it. Although

I suppose it will be Flynn Davis Fortune Chesterfield now." He closed his eyes for a moment, leaned his head back and tried to gather his roiling thoughts. "I almost understand why you didn't tell me at first, but after he was born…"

"I'm sorry, Charles. Really, I am." She placed a hand on his arm. The touch was light, but it reverberated through him. "I had a lot of resistance at first from my friends and family. Not only could no one believe I'd gotten pregnant, but they also didn't think I could handle a baby on my own. Not my coworkers, friends or even my parents." Flynn fidgeted in her arms and she drew her hand away from Charles to snuggle the baby closer, his eyes drifting shut again. "But I knew being a mother would change everything for me."

She gazed at Flynn, her eyes full of so much affection that Charles instinctively leaned closer, wanting to be a part of that kind of love.

"It did change me," she said. "It made me better and stronger, but I got used to being on my own. I started relying on myself and it felt like that was my only option. Until…"

"Until what?" Charles asked, so close now he could smell the vanilla scent of her shampoo.

"It's silly, but I was getting a haircut last month and saw a picture of you in an old tabloid magazine."

Charles grimaced. "Whatever the article said, I highly doubt it was true."

She laughed, and Charles watched as Flynn's eyes snapped open, focusing on her face. The boy seemed as fascinated by Alice as Charles felt. How did a baby form that bond so quickly? Did Charles have it in him to be any sort of father to this child?

"It was a photo of you holding your niece, Clementine. The magazine was from last year, so she was around Flynn's age in the picture. You looked so…" Alice searched his face, offered him another hopeful smile.

"Terrified out of my mind," he suggested.

"Natural," she corrected. "You looked natural holding the baby—like it made you happy."

"Little Clementine is a fine baby."

She shrugged. "It made me realize it wasn't fair to keep Flynn from you. Again, I'm sorry. For the shock and for not telling you earlier. Like I said, I don't expect anything from you."

He knew she meant the words as comfort, but they were like salt in an open wound. No one had ever expected anything from Charles. Nothing beyond a laugh, a free pint and a good time. For a long time, he'd liked it that way. But now…this was different.

"Would you like to hold him?" Alice asked gently.

He almost said no. Flynn wasn't a niece or nephew he could bounce on his knee, then hand back to a doting parent. *He* was the parent. Alice might think he looked like a natural, but he certainly didn't feel like one. Still, when she shifted toward him, Charles reached for the baby.

"Relax," Alice coached him. "You're doing fine."

Forcing his muscles to loosen, Charles held the baby close to his chest, cradled in the crook of his arm. Flynn yawned, stretched and blinked. His blue gaze, so familiar, yet all his own, met Charles's. At that moment, Charles felt his world rumble and shift. It wasn't like a lightning bolt or clap of thunder. But the energy inside him changed. Here was the meaning he'd been craving in his life, all wrapped up in one tiny, powder-scented package. He was holding *his son* in his arms.

He wrapped his arms tighter around the baby and placed a gentle kiss on Flynn's forehead.

Alice gasped when Charles kissed Flynn, her whole world suddenly spinning out of control.

Charles glanced up at her. "Did I do something wrong?"

She shook her head. "No, of course not. I just didn't think you'd to take to him so quickly. I thought…" She trailed off, knowing that everything she'd expected about Charles's reaction to finding out he had a son was insulting and, apparently, off the mark.

Obligation and a niggling sense of guilt had prompted her to call him when she'd found out he was visiting his family in Texas. But she hadn't realized what had stopped her from contacting him before that. It wasn't as much how he would respond to the knowledge of being a father, but Alice's reaction to Charles.

They'd spent only one night together, but she'd felt the overwhelming charge of attraction and longing as soon as she looked up and saw him standing in front of her today. He was just as handsome, looking almost formal and wholly British in his slim trousers, expensive loafers and dark, fitted shirt.

The temperature was beginning to rise as the sun drew higher in the sky, and Alice could feel a bead of sweat roll between her shoulder blades. Charles, on the other hand, looked as dashing and sophisticated as if he were ready to meet a foreign dignitary. He smelled delicious, expensive and spicy. The scent made her want to lean in closer to him and beg him to press his mouth to hers.

She was such a fool.

Charles likely hadn't given her a moment's thought in the past year, and she'd struggled to keep him out of her mind and, more annoyingly, her dreams. But Charles in the flesh was far more powerful than her fantasy version. To see him show such easy affection with her son—with *their* son—made Alice almost melt on the spot.

Unfortunately, it also made the future far more complicated, and she liked her simple life with Flynn.

"My father was a wonderful man," Charles told her, his gaze back on the baby. "The most honorable, good-hearted, kind person I've ever known. I couldn't ever hope to compare to him, but I want to follow his example. I'm going to do the right thing by Flynn, Alice. I promise you that much."

She nodded dumbly, unable to speak around the emotion rising thick and hot in her throat. Automatically, she reached for the baby, needing the weight of Flynn in her arms to settle her. Charles handed him to her, their fingers brushing as he did. She felt the touch all the way to her toes, her skin tingling with awareness. Needing to gain control of herself, Alice stood and gently placed Flynn back into his stroller. She strapped him into the infant seat and turned to Charles. "I should go," she said, "Thank you for meeting me and for being so good about all of this. I really don't—"

"Expect a call from me tomorrow," Charles interrupted, also standing. He slid the sunshade over Flynn and took a step toward Alice before stopping. "I have some plans to put into motion, papers to draw up." His fingers rested on the stroller handle as hers had earlier. His touch was confident, proprietary, and despite his devil-may-care attitude about life, Alice knew from

Charles's work with the tourism council that he was smart and cunning, with powerful connections on both sides of the Atlantic. Once he decided there was something he wanted, little could stop him from having it.

"If you change your mind, I understand," Alice said quickly, no longer sure what she wanted from her son's father. Afraid of both what he made her feel and the way he could change her life.

"I won't." He leaned forward, kissed her cheek in much the same way he'd kissed Flynn's forehead. The brush of his lips was gentle, sweet and utterly irresistible. Cue the melting once again. Great. Just when Alice needed to keep her wits about her, one innocent touch could turn her to mush. "Thank you, Alice," he said as he straightened. "For calling me. This morning has changed everything."

"Goodbye, Charles," she said, and gripped the stroller handle harder than necessary. He moved back and she turned for the path toward her car, his words echoing in her ears.

Yes, everything had changed. Now she wondered exactly what that would mean for her.

Chapter Three

"Why am I such an idiot?" she asked Meredith later that night. They were back in Alice's cozy apartment, and she'd just put Flynn down for the night.

"Something about a hot guy will do that to you." Meredith tipped her wineglass toward Alice. "Add a British accent to the mix, and it's no wonder your ovaries went into overdrive with Charlie Boy."

"He wants to be a father to Flynn," Alice told her friend with a small sigh. She brought her own glass to her lips but set it on the coffee table before taking a drink. Her head had been pounding since the meeting with Charles, and she didn't need anything to make it worse.

"Isn't that what you wanted?" Meredith asked, clearly confused.

"No...yes... I have no idea what I want," Alice admitted. "I'm so tired, I can't think straight."

Meredith gave her a sympathetic smile. "The transition back to work hasn't been an easy one."

"I love my job, but it's different now that I have Flynn. Everything is different." Her maternity leave had ended just over a month ago, and she'd returned to her job with the Texas Tourism Board, which was based out of Austin. She'd worked there for just over three years, and what Alice lacked in a gregarious, outgoing personality, she made up for in attention to detail, understanding the market and her ability to assess what people wanted out of a visit. But it was more difficult for those skills to shine through when she was chronically sleep deprived and always torn between being at work or at home with her son.

She'd modified her schedule so she could work from home two days a week, and had found a semiretired nanny, a sweet older woman, to watch Flynn another two days. Alice's mother took the baby one day a week. But Alice still got up before dawn most mornings to put in extra hours, and with Flynn's sometimes erratic sleeping patterns, she never felt rested. Her exhaustion was starting to take a toll, and Alice often felt like she was slogging through mud just to form a coherent thought.

"Charles had a right to know he has a child," she told Meredith, "but I never expected him to take to the idea so readily. Of course I want Flynn to know his father, but he's my son. Mine." Her voice caught, and she cleared her throat. "Flynn is my sole reason for being and now I'm going to have to share him. What if Charles wants partial custody? What if he takes Flynn to England for part of the year?" She knew she sounded irrational but couldn't help it. Being a mother was the best thing that had ever happened to her. She couldn't imagine a night

when she didn't tuck Flynn in bed or a morning without
a baby-scented snuggle to greet her.

"What if he wants the three of you to be a family?"
Meredith asked.

Alice snorted. "Don't be ridiculous. Charles has no
interest in me beyond Flynn. He barely remembered who
I was at first. Just another in his long list of conquests in
the bedroom." She drew her knees up to her chest and
rested her chin on them. "Not that I was much of a prize."

"Don't sell yourself short, Alice. You're not an awkward teenager anymore. In case you haven't looked in a
mirror in the past few years, you're gorgeous. Men stare
at you everywhere we go."

"They don't—"

"They do, but you don't notice."

"I noticed Charles," Alice admitted. "We only had
one night together and it's been over a year. I'm tired,
stressed and still have ten pounds of baby weight to lose.
The last thing on my mind is men. But I could barely
form a sentence this morning because of my reaction to
him. How am I supposed to remain calm and in control
when all I want is to…"

"Jump his bones?" Meredith suggested with a wink.

Alice laughed at the old-school expression, a welcome
break in the tension that seemed ready to consume her.
"I'm a mother now, Mer."

"Last time I checked, you're still a woman."

The funny thing was, the only time Alice had felt
like a woman recently was with Charles. He made her
feel alive and aware of herself in a different way than
normal. In a way that made her hot and itchy and longing for…more. It had to be something biological, like
pheromones. There was no other way to account for her

reaction to him. "Until I know how Charles wants to proceed, I can't let down my guard. Flynn is my first—my only—priority."

"Then you have to at least give Charles a chance." Meredith stood, picked up both their wineglasses. "For Flynn's sake."

Alice unfolded her legs and followed her friend to the kitchen, where Meredith set the glasses in the sink. "Thanks for listening. I needed a friend tonight."

"My pleasure, sweetie." Meredith hugged her. "I've got to go now. I'm meeting a few people for drinks at a bar downtown. Want to call a last-minute sitter and join us?"

Alice grimaced. "It's nearly nine."

"The night is young."

"Not for me. I'm exhausted and my alarm is already set for five tomorrow morning."

"I'll see you at the office, then," Meredith said.

Alice locked the door to her apartment behind her friend and sighed. Her mind drifted to Charles and what he might be doing tonight. Was he also at a bar downtown or out to dinner with a woman? He had no shortage of female companionship, and Alice knew she didn't stand a chance when compared to the women he usually favored. Of course, she'd see him again, thanks to Flynn, but Alice hated that she longed for more. Her attraction to him made her feel weak when what she needed was to be strong for her son.

She quietly let herself into Flynn's room. Her eyes adjusted to the darkness and she approached the crib. He slept on his back, his face turned toward her, and her heart swelled with love at how innocent he was. He deserved the best she could give him, which was why she worked so hard, put in extra hours and ignored her own needs. That's what mothers did for their children.

She'd wait to hear from Charles and concentrate on ignoring her feelings for the tall, handsome Englishman. Her only identity was that of a mother, and it was better for everyone if she didn't fool herself into thinking it could be anything else.

Charles lay in bed early the next morning, watching the windows of his hotel suite slowly brighten with dawn light. His sleep had been sporadic and fitful. He'd drift off, only to awake in a cold sweat minutes later. Wispy tendrils of panic had threatened to claim him in the dark, so many unspoken fears and regrets from his life coalescing into one important word.

Father.

Bloody hell.

What had he been thinking to tell Alice he wanted to be a part of Flynn's life? She'd seemed more than willing to let him off the hook. Shirking responsibility was Charles's specialty in life. He'd even made a successful career of taking the easy way out. He traveled, shook hands with dignitaries and the rich and famous. He attended parties and smiled for the cameras, and somehow that made him an asset to the British tourism industry.

His existence was so different than that of his siblings, with their businesses, philanthropic projects and seemingly endless supply of energy and work ethic. Even if the superficiality of his life had begun to chafe at his soul, it was what Charles did well. He knew he wouldn't fail at being a man about town. The stakes were too low for him to care that much. And if he didn't care, he couldn't be hurt. Wouldn't disappoint anyone.

Flynn and Alice were different. They upped the stakes in a manner that scared the hell out of him. Charles certainly knew people whose lifestyles hadn't been affected by parenthood. Friends of his from the exclusive schools he'd attended growing up hired nurses, nannies and housekeepers while they continued to party and travel with their society wives, leaving the care of the children to the hired help. It was a time-honored tradition in the British upper class but bore little resemblance to how Sir Simon and Lady Josephine had raised Charles and his siblings.

His parents had built their lives around the family, raising a tight-knit group of children with love, laughter and bucketfuls of patience.

Charles knew he'd been a particular challenge, always into mischief as a boy and usually pulling one or more of his siblings along with him. It was all in good fun, and as much as he pushed the limits of his parents' patience, he never once doubted their unconditional love.

He'd spent enough time with his siblings and their spouses to know they were raising their children with much the same philosophy. His family set the bar high, and this was the first time Charles felt the need to live up to those standards.

If only he knew how.

He didn't have the first clue about being an instant family man, and it wasn't just Flynn that scared him. The beautiful blonde from a year ago had occasionally flitted across his mind, leaving him with a satisfied smile and a trace of longing. Seeing Alice again had felt like a swift blow to the head, knocking him off his game and instantly breaking through the self-control he'd so carefully cultivated. He tried to tell himself it was simply because she was now the mother of his son, but it felt like something more. It felt as if she might be the answer to a question he hadn't even thought to pose.

He grabbed his phone off the nightstand and quickly texted Lucie. A part of him dreaded telling anyone in his family about this monumental development in his life, but they were bound to discover it sooner than later. One thing that came with having such a close family was the inability to keep anything secret.

But his younger sister had managed to keep her marriage to Chase Parker under wraps for ten years. Technically, Lucie had believed that the marriage had been annulled shortly after it had taken place, but still…

Lucie texted back almost immediately and agreed to meet him for breakfast in an hour. He forced himself out of bed, then took a hot shower in the hopes of reviving himself a bit. He was on his third cup of black coffee in the hotel restaurant when his sister sank into the chair across from him.

"To what do I owe the pleasure?" she asked, folding her hands in front of her on the table. "I thought you were heading to Horseback Hollow this morning."

"Plans changed," he said, his leg bouncing under the table. It probably hadn't been the best idea to over-caffeinate before this conversation.

"Official *royal* tourism business, I assume," Lucie said with a smirk. She took a drink of water from the goblet set at her place. None of his siblings ever tired of teasing him about the ad campaign.

"I have a son," Charles answered, the older brother in him slightly gratified when she choked and coughed, her eyes widening in shock as she lifted a napkin to her mouth.

"How... When... Who...?" Lucie looked as gob-smacked as Charles felt, but it was good to say the words out loud. Not that holding Flynn in his arms hadn't made it real, but he'd almost wondered if lightning might strike him down for actually claiming the boy as his own.

A waiter approached their table, and Charles glanced at the menu. "I'll have the eggs Benedict," he told the young man. "How about you, Luce?"

She didn't move but continued to stare at him, mouth agape.

"She'll have tea and the granola and yogurt, I believe."

With a curious glance at Lucie, the waiter nodded and walked away.

Charles picked up his coffee cup, then set it down again, as his head was still buzzing. He waved his fingers in front of his sister's face until she blinked. "Which question would you like answered first?"

Patting the napkin to her lips, she leaned forward. "How did this happen?"

He felt the corner of his mouth curve, since that was the exact question he'd first asked Alice. "The usual way."

Lucie blinked a few more times. "How old is the boy?"

"Four months."

"And the mother?"

"I don't know her exact date of birth, but I'd guess midtwenties."

"This is serious, Charles."

"Trust me, Lucie," he said, as he ran a hand through his hair, "I know that."

She gave the barest nod of acknowledgment. "Who is the mother?"

"Her name is Alice Meyers."

"The woman who called when we were out the other day?"

"Yes. She lives here in Austin and heard I was in town."

"Why hadn't she told you about the baby before now?"

He shrugged. "She didn't think I would want to be involved."

Lucie tilted her head, considering that.

"I'm not certain she even wants me involved," Charles continued. "She seems to be managing fine on her own."

"Are you sure…" Lucie trailed off as the waiter brought a small tea service to the table.

"That he's mine?" Charles finished when the waiter had left again. "Yes. His name is Flynn, and he looks just like me and quite a bit like Ollie when he was that age."

Lucie met Charles's gaze as she unwrapped a tea bag and poured steaming water over it. "Still…how well do you know this Alice Meyers? If she's one of your usual girls, you should have proof. There are tests—"

"Alice offered, but I refused." He took a deep breath as he thought about Alice's big eyes and sweet smile. "She wouldn't…there's no question. I'm the father."

"So what now?"

Charles had a minute to think about his answer as their food arrived. "I've put in a call to the family attorney," he said, then took a bite of egg. "The first order of business is making provisions for the boy."

"There's more to being a daddy than 'making provisions,' Charles." Lucie's tone was chiding.

"I understand that, but I have to start somewhere." He pointed his fork at his sister. "Cut me a bit of slack, Lucie. This was a shock, to say the least."

She nodded. "Well, if this Alice Meyers isn't asking for anything, then I suppose you have options."

"What kind of options?" Charles demanded, his breakfast suddenly churning in his stomach. He tossed his napkin over his barely eaten plate of food. "Are you suggesting that I ignore the responsibility I have to my son?" He said the words through clenched teeth, hating that they were exactly what he'd been thinking earlier. A child meant commitment, and everyone knew Charles didn't do commitment.

But he wanted to now. He wanted to be a decent father to Flynn. He wanted someone to believe he could.

"You wouldn't ignore it," Lucie said gently. "I'm fully aware of how you've lived to this point, Charles, but you are a good man in your heart. You're our father's son. You *will* make this work."

His sister's words were a salve on the wound of his self-doubt. Lucie was right. Charles might not have any idea of how to be a father, but as he'd told Alice, he'd had the best role model anyone could ask for in Sir Simon. Still, he wondered where to even begin. "He's so tiny," he said to Lucie. "Like a miniature old man. Only soft and cute."

Lucie grinned. "That's an interesting mental image. Do you have a picture?"

Charles shook his head. "I could barely remember my own name once I saw him, let alone to take a photo. But I'm staying in Austin and will get to know him."

"What about Alice?"

"I'll prove to her that I deserve to be part of Flynn's life, if that's what it takes."

"What I meant was, where does Alice fit into all of

this? Mothers and babies are kind of a package deal, you know. How do you feel about Alice?"

"Alice seems…" How did he describe his jumbled feelings for a woman he'd spent only one night with but couldn't get out of his mind? Alice was not just beautiful on the outside but a truly good person, someone who deserved to be loved and cherished. She was the kind of woman who produced thoughts of rings and bended knees and forever. Charles might be able to manage fatherhood, but that didn't make him a forever type of chap. "She's nice, Lucie. Far too nice for someone like me."

"You've always sold yourself short."

"I'm a realist," he argued. "I know who I am."

"You know who you've been up until now," she countered. "You're not in Britain, Charles. Trust me, Texas is the best place for a new start."

"One step at a time."

"Just promise me you'll get to know Alice as well as the baby."

He signaled for the check. "Of course. I'll be spending time with both of them. I can't very well take a baby gallivanting about town on my own."

"You know what I mean." Lucie rolled her eyes. "You have more walls surrounding you than the Tower of London. Get to know her, Charles, and let her know you. The real you, not only Bonnie Lord Charlie."

"Does that mean you believe there's more to me than 'the royal treatment'?" he asked. It was meant to be a joke but the question came out in an almost desperate tone.

"I know there is," Lucie answered just as gravely.

He gave a curt nod, hoping his sister was right.

Chapter Four

Alice finished giving Flynn his bottle just as the doorbell rang later that afternoon. Charles had texted in the morning, asking if he could stop by to talk about the next steps, and Alice had been teetering on the edge of panic ever since.

What did that mean? She knew she had rights as Flynn's mother, but was also aware that her meager resources were no match for the Fortune Chesterfield family's power and influence.

She placed the empty bottle in the sink and threw a burp cloth over her shoulder as she walked toward the door. Her legs grew heavier with each step, even though she'd donned her favorite wedge sandals, a black-and-white zebra-print pattern with sparkling crystals embedded in the ankle strap. Alice didn't need the extra height but somehow wearing heels always gave her a little jolt of confidence. And she needed all the confidence she could get to face Charles again.

She opened the door slowly, mentally steeling herself for the sight of the tall, dapper Brit. Unfortunately, not even a superhero-level force field could protect her from Charles. Today he wore dark trousers and a crisp tailored button-down shirt. He looked amazing. She bit down on her lip to keep a groan from escaping, and he flashed a quick, almost uncertain smile.

"Hullo, Alice." That accent should be illegal for the things it did to her insides. But before the requisite melting could start, Flynn let out a burp that would make a drunken sailor proud. Nothing like a bit of baby reflux for an icebreaker.

She rubbed a hand along Flynn's back and stepped away from the door. "Come on in." Then she glanced at the throng of bags and packages gathered at Charles's feet. "Did you rob a toy store?"

He gave her another smile and adjusted his shirt collar. "I hope you don't mind. I picked up a few necessities for the boy."

Flynn belched again and this time she could feel something warm soak into the cloth over her shoulder. She dipped her chin to look at Flynn, whose cheek was now resting in a puddle of spit-up formula. "Let me just clean him up," she said quickly, noting that Charles's expression was an equal mix of amusement and disgust.

She turned for the nursery and made quick work of cleaning Flynn, who gurgled and gazed at her. She changed his outfit, ridiculously wanting her son to make a good impression with Charles this afternoon. She realized if Charles did indeed decide to be a regular part of Flynn's life, he'd have to get used to the dirty work of taking care of a baby. Still, for now she wanted things to be easy.

By the time she returned to the apartment's small living area, it appeared that half the room was filled with toys and space-guzzling baby contraptions. Alice had purchased the bare essentials when she was pregnant, both to save money and because her two-bedroom apartment in the trendy neighborhood west of downtown and close to her work had a lot of charm but not much room.

"Is that a T-ball set?" she asked, balancing Flynn in one arm as she pointed to a package that held an oversize baseball and plastic T.

"Baseball is the American pastime," Charles told her. "I thought Flynn and I could learn together."

She couldn't help her smile. "It will be a few years before he's ready for a ball and glove."

"I have time," Charles answered, his tone serious. "I want you to know I'm here for the duration, Alice. I'll admit I have no idea what I'm doing." He gestured to the mass of packages on the floor, looking hopeful and utterly irresistible. "But I want to try, if you'll give me a chance."

The good news was she'd gone a whole five minutes without melting into a needy, longing puddle at Charles's feet. The bad news was, with one sentence, he'd completely turned her to mush. She nodded, not trusting her voice at the moment.

She knew he was talking about trying with Flynn, but Alice couldn't stop herself from wanting more. For a year she'd been fine, proud that she'd risen to the challenge of having a baby by herself, resolved to raise Flynn on her own.

Charles made her long for things a woman like her

couldn't expect to have. What he was offering had to be enough. It was the right thing for Flynn, and that's what was important. As much as she'd tried to convince herself otherwise, a boy needed his father. Her own dad was sweet, if a bit distant and bumbling, in the role of grandpa, much as he'd been as a father to her. But Henry Meyers, tenured professor of history at the University of Texas at Austin, was never going to teach Flynn to play baseball or how to catch a fish or any of the things men other than her father seemed to know by osmosis.

Charles, for all his formal British mannerisms and expensive suits, was a man's man. She'd seen pictures on the internet of him horseback riding and fly-fishing, things she wanted her son to learn if he was interested.

"As soon as I discovered I was pregnant," she said quietly, "my baby became my whole world. I'd do anything for Flynn. I thought it was right not to tell you, Charles. I figured you'd be like the rest of my family and friends, who thought I couldn't handle being a mother. They said I was too fragile, that it took strength and hard work to raise a child alone." She pressed a cheek to the top of Flynn's downy head. "I needed to prove to them, and to myself, that I could do it."

"Alice."

She shook her head. "You say you don't know what you're doing, but many new parents don't at the beginning. Even if you think you're prepared, if you've read every child-rearing book and article ever published, if every weekend has been filled with classes and workshops, nothing prepares you for the moment you hold the baby. Nothing truly prepares you to take that tiny bundle home, knowing you're responsible for another life.

I've learned a lot in just four months, and here's the one thing that can't be taught."

She took a deep breath, cleared her throat. "It's how to love someone. The reason parents work so hard is love. A life-altering, fierce and potent love for your baby that makes all the sleepless nights and fear and doubt worth it." She stepped closer, watched Charles's blue eyes widen as he glanced between her and Flynn. "You said your father was wonderful, and I know you come from a close-knit family. You know how to love, Charles. I don't expect it to happen overnight, but I know you'll make a good father. I believe Flynn is lucky to have you." She smiled and held the baby toward him.

Charles didn't realize how much he needed to have someone believe in him until Alice said the words out loud. This woman, whom he barely knew, seemed to see into the heart of him, past his superficial facade and the walls he'd constructed that everyone else assumed made him who he was. She slew him with her honesty—a unique mix of vulnerability and strength.

He reached for Flynn, even as he wanted to scoop up Alice, too. His fingers itched to pull them both close and hope some of her goodness transferred to him. He settled for the baby, aware that Alice had let him into her life for the sake of the boy.

Supporting Flynn's body in the crook of his elbow, he placed a hand on the back of the baby's head and lifted him. Flynn's deep blue gaze focused on Charles, glancing from his nose to his mouth, then finally settling on his eyes. They watched each other for a moment before Flynn squirmed and his tiny, rosebud mouth curved into a small smile.

Charles hitched in a breath, knocked for an emotional loop at how much one tiny smile could mean to him. "I think he has gas," he muttered.

Alice laughed. "He's smiling at you. He's a happy baby, Charles." She stifled a yawn. "Not much of an overnight sleeper, but very happy."

He stood there, transfixed by the baby in his arms. "What do I do now?"

She laughed again. "Talk to him. Bounce him. He's just like your niece and nephews."

"He's different," Charles whispered. "He's mine."

Alice sank to her knees on the floor. "Is there anything in this generous pile of gifts that he can use before he's a toddler?"

Right. The toys. The reminder snapped Charles out of his reverie. "We should be able to find something. What do you think, Flynn?" He lifted the baby closer, blew a tickling breath against his neck and was rewarded with a gurgling laugh. It was the best sound he'd ever heard.

"Try that," he said, pointing to one of the larger shopping bags. He lowered himself next to her, turning Flynn to sit on his forearm, the baby's back and head resting against Charles's chest. "I got an activity gym. The colors are glaringly bright, but the saleslady assured me it's top-of-the-line and perfect for a four-month-old." He glanced at her. "Unless you have one already?"

"Not yet," Alice said with a shy smile. She reached for the bag but stopped as Flynn let out a determined grunt.

Charles glanced down at the boy, whose face turned bright red. "I think he's digested the bottle," he told Alice as he quickly held out Flynn with two hands. The baby kicked and gurgled some more, but there was no mistaking the smell radiating from his back end.

"Let me," Alice said quickly, scrambling to her feet. "We'll be back in a minute."

Charles let out a relieved breath as she disappeared into a bedroom with Flynn. Twenty-four hours a dad, and Charles wasn't sure he was quite ready for nappy duty. Instead he pulled the activity gym out of the box and fastened the toys to the arches that crisscrossed over the soft mat. By the time Alice returned with a fresh-scented Flynn, Charles was just putting batteries into the motorized mobile piece of the play set.

Alice crouched down and lay Flynn on his back under the arches. The boy immediately kicked his feet and swatted at the dangling toys with his hands.

"He's got the hang of it already," Charles said proudly. "Smart lad. Takes after his…" He paused as Alice arched a brow. "Both his parents."

"Of course," she agreed with a grin.

He loved making Alice smile and was surprised to find himself content to watch Flynn play with the toys, entranced by the joyful noises the baby made. Alice settled on the floor, stretching her legs in front of her, her back resting against one of the chairs in the small family room. Charles wished he could pull her to his side, tuck her up against him and feel her breathing, but he also knew what he wanted from her was less platonic than simple companionship.

He moved to the far side of the activity gym and traced one finger along the leather strap at her ankle. "I love these shoes," he told her.

"Me, too." She flexed and pointed her foot a few times. "I'd have a lot more savings in my retirement account if I didn't love shoes so much."

"You don't have to worry about a retirement account

any longer," he said. "I'm going to take care of you and Flynn."

Immediately she moved, drawing her feet up underneath her. "That's not what I was suggesting. You don't owe me anything, Charles."

"You're the mother of my child, Alice. Do you really think I'd ignore that?"

"I didn't seek you out for financial support."

"Which doesn't change the fact that I have it to give."

She bit down on her lip, moved closer to Flynn and softly stroked one of his tiny feet. "Are you going to try to take him away from me?"

"No," Charles answered immediately, taking her hand in his. "Alice, look at me."

She glanced up, her gaze wary.

"Why would you think that?"

"Because you're rich and powerful and British. Texas isn't your home. I know that."

He chuckled softly. "It's quickly becoming my second home, especially since most of my family lives here now."

"But you'll return to England at some point."

He nodded.

"I can't be separated from Flynn. He's too young. He's all I have."

"That isn't my intention, Alice." As much as he'd loved making her smile, Charles equally hated that he'd caused the pain he saw in her eyes now. "I've changed my plans so I'll be in Austin for three weeks. After that, I'll need to figure out the next step. But I'm not going to take Flynn from you. I promise, Alice."

She gave a shaky nod, swiped under her eye. He

shifted closer to her and traced the pad of his thumb along her moist cheek. "No tears, sweetheart."

"I'm sorry," she said automatically. "I'm tired and…"

"No apologies, either." He dipped his head until his lips barely brushed hers. "We're in this together. The three of us are a team."

"A team?" she said, the husky note in her voice making him nip the corner of her mouth.

"Team Fortune Chesterfield," he whispered, and pressed his lips to hers. Her mouth was soft and yielding, molding to his without question. The taste of her was new and yet familiar, and all the memories of their night together came flooding back to him. The way she'd touched him, her innocence the most erotic thing he'd ever encountered… His fingers trailed through her hair, which was soft as spun silk. He remembered how it felt to have those thick, blond waves fanned out across his chest as she slept. Her tongue touched his, hesitantly, as if she wasn't sure whether he wanted the kiss to deepen.

There were no words for what Charles wanted from Alice. His need was so elemental, the potential ramifications so jumbled in his mind that he could barely form a coherent thought. His body grew heavy with desire. Desire he understood. Then he felt something in his heart, a slight shift from normal, and a skipped beat that had him tearing his mouth away from hers. In all Charles's many interactions with women, his protected heart had never come into play. No one had ever come close to breaching his defenses.

Until now.

Until Alice.

"I have to go," he said as he lurched to his feet. "There's a… I need to… I'll call you tomorrow."

She stared up at him as if he had just sprouted a horn from his forehead. Her fingers pressed to her mouth like she couldn't believe it had, moments earlier, been crushed under his. What the hell was wrong with him? Alice told him she believed in him, gave him a chance to be a father and first thing out of the gate he practically mauled her. So much for his legendary charm and experience. He felt like a randy schoolboy with his first crush.

"Thank you for the gifts," she said after a moment.

"Of course." He ran a hand through his hair even as he backed toward the door of her apartment. "I can bring more. If there's anything you need—"

"No." She glanced at Flynn, who was now dozing under the activity gym, and then stood. "You've done more than enough, Charles." Her hands were clenched at her sides in tight fists. If he had to guess, she was trying hard not to physically push him from her home. That was no less than what he deserved.

"I'll call you," he repeated, and turned for the door. But before opening it, he swung back, dropped to his knees and reached for Flynn's chubby hand. "Goodbye, little man," he whispered. "Sweet dreams."

Chapter Five

Alice stood under the shade of an elm tree in front of her building the next afternoon, watching as a sleek Mercedes sedan pulled to the curb. True to his word, Charles had called that morning and asked to see her and Flynn again, suggesting he bring lunch to her apartment.

Unfortunately, Alice didn't trust herself alone with the handsome Brit after yesterday's kissing fiasco. Yes, she wanted a father for her son. But could she and Flynn ever be enough for him? She'd told herself at the start of all this that her needs were secondary to those of her son, but she was having trouble convincing her body. It had felt so right when Charles touched his lips to hers, and she'd wanted to sink into him and revel in the feel of her body thrumming back to life.

It had been silly to believe that Charles would want anything more from her than access to Flynn. What could someone like her possibly offer a man like him? The same doubts had plagued her during her pregnancy, contributing to her long list of reasons for not contacting him.

If she'd had any hopes about him wanting her in that way, they'd been shattered when he'd broken their embrace like she'd tried to eat him alive and he had one chance for escape. She'd gone for more than two decades without a man before Charles, and over a year since their night together. Maybe that's why her need for him seemed to overpower her.

Although she was rarely alone, with Flynn to look after, motherhood added a level of isolation to her already quiet life that she hadn't expected. Still, she had no intention ruining the fragile bond Charles had with Flynn just because she was the modern day equivalent of a dried-up spinster.

With that in mind, public outings with Charles seemed the most prudent course of action. But they still needed to maintain some level of anonymity. According to Charles, most people believed he'd gone to Horseback Hollow, as was his original plan. That gave them some time, but although Austin wasn't as overtly overrun with cowboys as Dallas or Houston, Charles didn't exactly blend in as a local. Alice hoped to remedy that today.

"Tell me again where we're going," Charles said as he approached her on the sidewalk. He wore a fitted black sweater, even though the temperature was hovering in the midseventies, and dark, tapered trousers. Even before he uttered a word, anyone within a block could tell he wasn't American.

"To the mall," she said. She held Flynn's infant seat

between them, needing every bit of physical distance she could manage.

"As in a shopping mall?"

Alice almost laughed at the words rolling off his tongue in that crisp accent. "Barton Creek Square isn't far from here, and you need a new wardrobe."

He ran a hand over the front of his sweater and arched an eyebrow. "Is there something wrong with my clothes?"

"Not if you want to constantly be recognized while you're in Austin," she told him. "You dress like you're British."

"I *am* British."

"Which is why we're going to turn you into an American for a few weeks." She smiled and stepped away from the building. "Trust me, Charles."

"I'm not wearing Wranglers," he mumbled, and she did laugh.

"No Wranglers," she agreed. "But at least one ten-gallon hat."

He shot her a horrified glance.

"I'm kidding." Alice found that she enjoyed teasing Charles. "Austin's fashion style is fairly casual and, because of the college and the music scene, it's less 'cowboy' than a lot of places in Texas. You'll be fine." She started for the walkway next to her building. "My car's in the lot around back."

"We can take mine."

"You don't have a car seat base."

He flashed her a proud smile. "I do, and I had it installed at the fire station the hotel concierge recommended."

She sucked in a breath, trying not to let her heart

be influenced by the thoughtfulness of that gesture. He lifted the car seat out of her hands, their fingers brushing.

"Hullo there, little man," he said to Flynn as he tipped back the sunshade. Flynn gurgled in response.

"I need to grab his stroller from the trunk of my car." She shrugged at Charles's questioning glance. "There's not a lot of room in the apartment, so I keep it in the car when I'm not using it."

He considered that for a moment. "A boy needs a yard to romp in, Alice."

"Flynn has a while to go before the 'romping' stage begins."

"If you'd let me—"

"My apartment is fine." She held up a hand. "One step at a time. Please."

"One step at a time. Let's drive around back to your car." He hit the remote start on the key fob and then clicked the infant carrier into the base waiting in his back seat. This was the first time she'd gotten in a car with her son and not been driving since her father brought her home from the hospital after Flynn's birth.

Charles held open the door and she slipped into the buttery leather seat, stowing the diaper bag at her feet.

"Do you always wear heels?" he asked, leaning over the top of the door.

"Whenever possible," she admitted. "These are low for me." Today she'd gone casual with a pair of polka-dot espadrilles with a stacked one-inch heel.

"I like them," he said simply, but the intensity in his eyes as they raked over her body made awareness whisper across her skin.

"Thanks," she murmured as he shut the door.

She concentrated on breathing as he came around the

front of the car, but that didn't help her muddled senses. The Mercedes was new, but the barest hint of Charles's scent lingered in the air. It wound around her brain until she felt like she might lose control, a feeling that only intensified when he climbed in and curled his long fingers around the steering wheel.

"Are you hot?" he asked, reaching forward to adjust the temperature control on the dash.

Alice almost choked on her own tongue. Was she hot? If he knew what she was feeling right now, he'd dump her and Flynn on the sidewalk in a minute. "Fine," she managed to reply in a normal tone.

They pulled around back and retrieved the stroller before heading toward Barton Creek Square. The upscale shopping center was only about ten minutes from her apartment.

"Of all the times I've visited the States," Charles said with a wry grin, "I've managed to avoid stepping into an American mall."

"Until now."

He winked at her. "Only for you, Alice."

She actually laughed at the absurdity of that statement. Now that she was becoming used to Charles being in close proximity, she began to relax. Driving to a mall was far less intimate than sitting together in her small apartment, even if it gave her the mistaken sense that somehow the three of them were a real family. Putting those dangerous thoughts aside, she pointed the edge of the mall out to Charles. "There's an underground parking garage near Nordstrom. That's a central starting point."

He nodded. "Even I've heard of Nordstrom."

"What do you normally do during your visits?"

"I see friends and my family. Texas is relatively new

for me. Before my mother discovered she was a Fortune, I'd spent most of my time on the coasts."

"Was being part of the Fortunes a big adjustment?"

"In some ways." Charles steered the sedan down the ramp of the multilevel parking structure. "But we've always been a big family, so having more cousins has been nice. None of us enjoy the additional notoriety that comes with the Fortune name, but we can deal with it."

"I heard that Kate Fortune is still in Austin. I saw a picture of her on the local news last week. She certainly is a walking advertisement for her youth serum."

His gaze was hooded as he glanced over. "I haven't met her yet."

"It's probably just a matter of time," Alice offered, wondering why she felt the need to placate Charles on the subject of Kate Fortune.

"We'll see." He pulled into an empty spot near the elevator on the second level and shifted the car into Park. "My sister Lucie told me Kate has been meeting with members of the Fortune extended family because she's looking for the right person to take over her company when she retires."

"That makes you a candidate?"

He shook his head. "Not yet. I've been in Austin almost a week and I've heard nothing from her. Not that I want to run a cosmetics company..."

"But you want the chance to say no."

One side of his mouth curved. "I'll admit, it pricks my ego not to be considered. Foolish, right?"

"Not at all." Alice understood how it felt to be overlooked, and as hard as it was to believe she had that in common with this handsome, dashing man, she knew that the pain of Kate Fortune's disregard went deeper than simple ego. "You'd be an excellent choice."

"Honestly, I have no desire to work with Fortune Cosmetics." He paused, tapped one hand on the steering wheel, then turned to her. "But what makes you think I could do it?"

She gave him a genuine smile. "You're smart and great with people. You have sharp instincts and I think you'd be a good manager."

He snorted. "I can barely manage my social calendar."

"That's what you want people to believe," Alice answered, shaking her head. "Because it's easier than admitting that you care. But you do, Charles. I watched you at the conference last year."

"I watched you, too, Alice." His voice was pitched low and she realized he was trying to distract her.

"Stop," she said, poking him in the arm. "This is serious."

He blinked at her. "I try to avoid being serious whenever possible. Everyone knows that about me."

"That's your mask, but there's more to you. No one can be as carefree as you act and still be successful without working very hard at it. You knew exactly what to say at the conference to put people at ease. You listened to what they wanted in a vacation and understood how to talk about England in a way that made it personal to each of them."

She hefted the diaper bag onto her lap, needing a distraction to stop thinking how personal she'd gotten with Charles after the conference. "Those were tourism professionals," she couldn't help but add. "They're practically immune to a sales pitch, even a very good one. But no one is immune to you, Charles."

He stared at her for several long moments and the nonchalance so often in his eyes dropped away for a moment, revealing a different man than the one the public knew. A man Alice could easily fall for if she wasn't careful.

"Not even you?" he asked.

She gave a startled laugh. "I'm a mother now. I don't count." Before he could weigh in on that pronouncement, she opened her door and climbed out. "We should get moving. Flynn will need to eat in about an hour and he usually gets fussy before that."

The air in the parking garage was sticky and stifling, and Alice quickly unfastened the car seat as Charles pulled the stroller out of the trunk. He didn't say anything as they walked toward the entrance of the mall, a burst of cool air greeting them when the automatic doors opened. Alice babbled on about the layout of the stores, the best options in the food court and the wonder that was the Nordstrom shoe department.

Charles listened but most of his attention was focused on maneuvering Flynn's stroller through the clusters of shoppers. Sunday afternoon was prime shopping time, and Alice wanted to find him some new clothes before he was spotted. The last thing she needed splashed across the local paper was a picture of Charles pushing Flynn's stroller.

"Here we are," she said as they came to a small storefront.

Charles squinted up at the sign. "This isn't Nordstrom."

"It's better if we start here. Marc & Cross is a Texas chain. They have stores in Austin, Dallas and San Antonio."

He glanced at the burly mannequins in the window, dressed as if they were going on some kind of hip cattle drive, then back at Alice. "You do a lot of shopping here?"

"No," she said around a giggle. "But I have friends who do."

"Boyfriends?" Charles's eyes narrowed.

She shook her head. "Friends who are guys."

"What's the difference?"

"I never… We didn't…you know." She wrapped her fingers around his upper arm and immediately regretted it. His biceps was hard and she could feel the warmth radiating from his skin.

"I'm certain they wanted to," Charles said, stubbornly staying right where he was. She tugged again. "I bet you had men lined up around the block."

"Hardly." She let go of his arm to walk into the store. He followed with the stroller. "I was such a late bloomer, I may have missed my chance entirely." She thought about her miserable love life before Charles and the condom that had languished in her purse for almost two years. The whole reason she now had Flynn. "We're not here to talk about me. We're getting clothes for you." She started for a rack near the front of the store, but Charles grabbed her wrist, sliding his fingers down her hand until they laced with hers.

"If that's the case, the men in Austin are complete prats." He grinned when she squinted. "Fools. They are complete fools, Alice."

"All of them but you," she whispered, then clasped a hand over her mouth. She hadn't meant to say the words out loud.

Charles's grin widened. "All of them but me," he

agreed. "Now what would you pick out that doesn't make *me* look like a prat?"

She started with a couple pairs of jeans, one a dark wash and another more faded. Both were boot cut, which Charles thought was ridiculous since he didn't own boots.

"Next stop is the Nordstrom shoe department," she informed him.

"My credit card is trembling with anticipation," he retorted.

She also picked out several shirts, both long and short sleeved, and a few pairs of shorts, since the temperature was going to only get hotter as spring progressed. One of the salesclerks took the clothes to a dressing room, and Alice couldn't help but notice the way the woman's eyes lingered on Charles. He seemed oblivious, and Alice figured basking in female attention was a daily occurrence for this far-too-attractive Fortune.

He shuddered as she handed him a baseball cap. "You can't possibly expect me to put that on my head."

"It's better than a cowboy hat, and it's good cover." She stepped toward him. Despite her height, she needed to stretch onto her tiptoes to place the hat on his head. She adjusted it, then brushed back the hair that curled at his neck.

His blue eyes darkened and he bent his head toward hers. So much for being safe in public. The bill of that baseball cap bumped her forehead at the same time Flynn let out a hungry squawk from his stroller.

Alice jumped away from Charles, knocking into a display of logo T-shirts. "You need shirts," she said, and blindly grabbed a few, shoving them toward him. "And Flynn needs to eat."

Charles took the shirts but watched her as she un-strapped the baby and lifted him from his carrier. "Do you need help?"

"I've got instant formula in the diaper bag." She hefted the sack in one arm, balancing Flynn in the other. "You try on everything. The food court is just across the way. We'll wait for you there."

Charles moved in front of her, lifted the diaper bag off her shoulder. "I'll get you settled first," he said, dropping a gentle kiss on the top of Flynn's head. It was a sweet gesture but also brought him close enough to whisper into her ear, "Unless you'd like to join me in the fitting room?"

"I…no," she blurted, and squeezed Flynn tighter. The boy let out a cry and the corners of his mouth turned down in a trembling pout that Alice knew indicated a full-blown wail wasn't far behind.

"Someday," Charles said smoothly, and turned for the back of the store.

Two weeks ago it would have seemed impossible to Charles that he could spend a thoroughly enjoyable afternoon in a temperature-controlled, fluorescent-lit shopping mall. But everything about being with Alice and Flynn shifted his preconceived notions about life. He had a suspicion that any activity done in the beautiful blonde's company would make for a better time than he'd had in years. Of course, the activities Charles most wanted to partake in with Alice weren't fit to even think about while he was bouncing his son on his knee, but he couldn't seem to stop his mind from wandering to thoughts of kissing her again.

After the first store, she'd convinced him to change into a pair of jeans and the Texas Longhorns T-shirt he'd purchased. The baggy denim and soft cotton felt foreign against his skin, but he had to admit he blended in better with the other men being led around the mall by their wives and girlfriends. He'd even gotten a pair of round-toed Western boots at Alice's beloved Nordstrom. He actually liked the weight of the shoes and was tempted to take a picture of himself to send to his siblings in Horseback Hollow. They wouldn't believe Charles dressed as an American.

His reward had been buying a pair of the sexiest shoes on the planet for Alice. She'd refused at first, but as soon as he saw the pair of strappy heels he'd wanted to see Alice in them. The more time he spent with her, the better he understood how men for so long had overlooked her.

Her pale blond hair and delicate features were gorgeous, but she had the ability to almost become invisible when other people were around. Her natural reserve and shyness made her shrink in on herself to the point that no one noticed her. Charles would have found it difficult to believe, since he could barely take his eyes off her, but in every store today the salespeople looked past her to him. She seemed to expect it, and the more it happened, the more Alice retreated.

The juxtaposition of the timid woman and the overtly sensual heels drove Charles crazy. The fact that he was the only man on the planet who knew that, underneath her shy exterior, Alice was just as passionate as the shoes would suggest just about sent him over the edge. He'd insisted she try on the red satin heels. The straps that wound around her ankles gave the impression that her feet were a tantalizing gift to be opened. Even with her wearing a crisp white T-shirt, and jeans rolled to her calves, her legs in those shoes were the most arousing thing he'd ever seen.

"They're too much," she argued, glancing at the price on the box.

"You're getting them." He jiggled Flynn on his knee, both hands supporting the baby, for Flynn's sake as well as to ensure that Charles didn't grab Alice and ravish her in the middle of the department store.

"I don't have an occasion to wear them." She sighed. "Since Flynn, my minuscule social life has become downright nonexistent."

"We'll find a place." Charles smiled at the salesclerk. "I'll take the heels and the boots," he told her, and handed over his credit card. When the woman walked away, he pointed at Alice. "Admit it, you love them."

She wrinkled her nose but grinned. "I do. I may just walk around the house tonight in my pajamas and heels because I love them that much."

"Any chance your pajamas are silk and lace?"

"Plain cotton flannel," she said with a snort, slipping her feet back into her espadrilles. "Not interesting at all."

"Invite me over," he coaxed. "I'll be the judge of that." Flynn waved his hands and kicked his feet. "Even the lad agrees."

Her face softened as she looked at Flynn. Charles could watch Alice watch their son for hours, marveling at the love shining in her eyes. Did all fathers feel this way about their child's mother? He was pretty sure Sir Simon had about Josephine. But his parents had been in love, and Charles barely knew Alice. It couldn't be anything more than the novelty of their situation.

"Charles—" she began, but broke off when his phone rang.

She scooped up Flynn as Charles pulled the phone from his pocket and glanced at the screen. His brother

Brodie. He sent the call to voice mail but a moment later the phone rang again. This time it was Jensen. Even as the phone rang, his text message alert sounded. "Damn," he muttered.

"Emergency?" Alice asked.

"To some people," he replied. In the midst of the barrage from his other siblings, Lucie texted to apologize for letting slip the news about Flynn and Alice. So much for his sister's ability to keep a secret. "I should probably deal with this." Charles held up his phone.

"No problem," Alice said immediately. "Flynn and I can walk—"

Did she really think he'd just desert her? It made him all the more frustrated at the intrusion when the result was Alice feeling insecure around him. "I'll drive you home first."

"I don't want to be a bother. If—"

"Alice, you aren't a bother." He realized his tone was harsher than he'd meant when she flinched. What was a bother were his nosy siblings. He took a step toward her. "I want to be with you and Flynn," he said gently. "Our son is my priority."

For some reason, his words made her hold the baby a little tighter to her chest. Charles wanted to question her but his phone rang again. "I'm silencing this thing until we're out of here. Let me sign the receipt and then we'll head for the car."

"I need to see to Flynn's diaper," she told him, looking almost apologetic. "There's a family restroom on the first floor."

"Then I'll bring the car from the garage and pick you up out front."

She nodded and placed the baby back in his carrier.

Charles watched her walk toward the elevator before finishing his purchase, collecting the shopping bags and starting for the car. He could feel the continuous vibration of his phone against his hip. His irritation grew by the second.

Whatever this was with Alice was too new to share with his family, as much as he loved them. He certainly didn't welcome their opinion on what kind of father he'd make. He could imagine what they'd have to say about that.

He pulled the car in front of the mall entrance and then helped Alice with the car seat and stroller. They were both silent on the way to her apartment, and Charles wished he could get back the cozy playfulness of the afternoon.

She practically jumped out of the sedan as he parked in front of her building. "I'm sorry for my foul mood," he told her as he took the stroller from the trunk. Where was his gift for charm when he needed it? "Let me walk you upstairs."

"It's fine." She clicked the car seat into place on top of the stroller. "You don't owe me an explanation, Charles. You don't owe me anything."

That might be true, but it wasn't what he wanted. His phone vibrated again. "Bloody hell, they're persistent." He scrubbed his palm across his jaw. "I've got to head out of town for a day. I'll see you when I get back." He bent his knees so he could look her in the eyes. "Right?"

Her rosy lips pressed together. "I don't expect—"

"No." He held a fingertip to her mouth. "I can't hear one more time that you don't expect anything from me. It's a refrain in my life that grows more tiresome by the hour." He leaned forward and replaced his finger with his mouth, giving her a kiss that he hoped promised her what he couldn't put into words just yet. "I'll see you soon, Alice."

She nodded, an adorable blush coloring her cheeks.

"Be good for your mum, little man," he said to Flynn, then climbed back into his car. He waited until he'd turned the corner from Alice's street, then pulled over to the curb. He quickly sent a group text to Brodie, Oliver, Jensen and Amelia.

Enough with the sodding messages. I'll be at the Horseback Hollow Cantina tomorrow at noon. Anyone with questions can meet me there.

Only a few seconds passed before the messages flooded in. Looked as if there would be a crowd of British Fortunes at lunch tomorrow.

Chapter Six

Alice didn't bother knocking on her parents' front door that night. She'd had Sunday dinner at their house every week since she'd moved out during her pregnancy.

At the time, both her mom and dad had begged her to stay. Although it had been a shock, her mother had taken the news of Alice's pregnancy better than her father. Lynn Meyers had mostly seemed worried that Alice wouldn't be able to keep herself and the baby safe and healthy if she went to live on her own.

She couldn't exactly blame her mother for worrying. Alice had lived at home all her life, even through four years at the University of Texas and once she started working for the tourism board. None of her friends had believed she was content to remain in her childhood bedroom, but Alice hadn't been motivated to leave until Flynn. Once she'd felt the baby move inside her, she'd started to resent her mother's well-meaning suggestions. Alice had needed to prove that she was strong enough to raise Flynn on her own, so she had put down the deposit on her small apartment two months before he'd been born.

Her father hadn't said a word when she moved out, which wasn't much different than how he'd been most of her life. Henry Meyers loved her, but he was far more interested in the details of the history of American immigration than his daughter's life. He hadn't questioned her story about the pregnancy being a result of a one-night stand, even though her mother continued to dig for more details about the father's identity.

There was no way she was going to reveal Bonnie Lord Charlie as Flynn's father to her parents. Meredith had a difficult enough time believing Alice could have caught the eye of the handsome Brit. Even if her mom and dad accepted the news, she wasn't ready to disclose her connection to Charles.

Her mom scooped up Flynn from his car seat as soon as Alice walked into the kitchen. Lynn cooed and cuddled the baby and even Alice's father fussed over him. It gave Alice a bit of confidence to remember that even if Charles didn't remain an active presence in Flynn's life, she had a family who loved her boy.

They ate the spaghetti dinner her mother had cooked and then Alice cleared the table while her mom fed Flynn a bottle and her father headed for his study.

"It feels like he changes every time I see him," Lynn said as Flynn's fingers curled around one of hers.

"He was almost sixteen pounds when I took him in for his four-month checkup last week." Alice stacked bowls and plates in the dishwasher as she spoke. "The doctor said he can try cereal before the end of the month."

"I wish you were still living here," her mother said gently. "I could help so much more. You look tired, sweetie."

Alice felt her fingers tighten around a glass. "I'm fine, Mom. He still isn't sleeping through the night. The pediatrician thinks solid food might help."

"I worry about you, Alice. Between work and caring for Flynn, there's no time for you. If you didn't have to work so many hours—"

"I love my job," Alice said, vigorously scrubbing the pasta pot before setting it on the dish drainer to dry. "And I love Flynn. I'm balancing the two of them the best I can. It's not an option to work less or else I can't pay for the babysitter and my apartment. You know that."

"But if you lived at home—"

"Not going to happen."

"Or had a husband…"

Alice dried her hands on a towel and went to sit at the table. Flynn had just finished his bottle and nuzzled his grandmother's shoulder as Lynn patted his back.

"Mom, I'm doing okay. Really."

"I know," her mother answered with a tender smile. "I'm proud of you, Alice. You're handling the responsibility of being a single mom better than I could have imagined. But it's hard for me to see you alone through all of this."

Alice thought of the time she'd spent with Charles in the past couple days. Being with him made even the mundane chores of parenting seem fun. Yes, she wanted more of that, but…

"There's something you're not telling me," her mother said suddenly, narrowing her eyes.

Alice blinked and tried to school her features. "No. It's nothing."

"It's a man," Lynn whispered.

"How do you…"

"Call it a mother's instinct," she continued, clearly perking up at the thought of a man in Alice's life. "Have you reconnected with Flynn's father?"

"I told you, I don't have a relationship with Flynn's father."

"At the time I believed you." Flynn burped and Lynn wiped a bit of spit-up from his chin. "But I can tell it's different now. Something, or someone, is on your mind. You were distracted during dinner. You listened to your father's thoughts on the instability of early colonial society without once suggesting that he start living in the present."

"It doesn't matter," Alice said quickly, but knew her mother could read through the blatant lie. Charles did matter, far more than she'd expected him to in such a short time. She wanted to believe him when he told her he'd be part of their son's life for the long haul, but it was difficult to discount his playboy reputation. "He's… Flynn's father is not the kind of man to commit to anyone."

"But he's the man you want?"

Alice sighed. "Nothing is going to come of it, Mom."

Lynn snuggled her grandson against her chest and Flynn's eyes drifted closed. "You're young, Alice. Just because you're a mother doesn't mean you don't have needs of your own."

"What I *need* is to take care of my baby." Alice stood

and lifted a sleeping Flynn from her mother's arms. "He's everything to me."

"You should have someone to take care of *you*, sweetie." Lynn stood and pressed a kiss to Alice's cheek and then Flynn's. "I'm not going to make you tell me who this man is, but I want you to know that I'm here if you need to talk. I know that your father and I were overprotective, and I probably still am, but you're a big girl now and I'm proud of you."

"Thanks, Mom." Tears pricked the back of Alice's eyes. "A baby might be exhausting, but it's a lot simpler, you know?"

Her mother gave a soft chuckle. "Life is complicated, relationships especially. Whoever this man is, if he could commit, do you see a future with him?"

Alice wanted a future with Charles with a longing that made her weak in the knees. But she was too practical to believe there was a chance of that happening. She couldn't hold a candle to the women he was used to, and the mundane reality of raising a child would never maintain his interest. "No," she whispered, and squeezed shut her eyes to keep from crying.

Immediately she was wrapped in a tight, motherly embrace. "I'm sorry, Alice." They stood in the kitchen for several minutes, Alice drawing strength from her mom until her breathing was back to normal.

Lynn drew away, ran a finger across Flynn's chubby cheek. "Whoever this man is, he's missing out on quite a prize."

Alice didn't have the heart to explain that Flynn's father might be keen on the baby, just not her. It felt weak and pathetic, when she should be thrilled and grateful that Charles was taking an interest in his son. That had been her goal from the first, and she couldn't let her feelings for Charles make her lose sight of that.

"We'll be fine." She had to believe that was true. Charles had gone to Horseback Hollow, so she had time to regain her emotional equilibrium before he returned. So far her intention of keeping her heart out of the mix had been a total failure, but she had to try harder.

Flynn was her whole reason for being, so how hard could it be to keep her interactions with Charles focused on the baby? Maybe she'd let things get too close too fast. Charles wanted to get to know Flynn, but there was no need to rush things. Maybe if she put the brakes on the time she spent with Charles, it would be easier to remember that the only reason he was in her life was the son they shared.

She was busy and tired, so it would probably make sense if she limited their contact to the weekends. Alice was a master at compartmentalizing her life. That seemed like a perfect solution to her trouble with Charles.

She kissed her mother goodbye and gave her father a hug, packed Flynn into her car and headed for home. She and her baby were a team. Team Meyers, not Team Fortune Chesterfield. Even if her team made her feel empty, it was best for everyone that she go it alone.

By the time Charles walked into the Horseback Hollow Cantina Monday afternoon, he was hot, tired and completely irritated by his siblings' interference in his life. It was nearly a six-hour drive from Austin to the quaint town that had become home to so much of his family. He'd left before sunrise and before he was halfway there had grown weary of the endless view of sky, livestock pastures and fields.

The long car ride had been somewhat productive, as he'd spent much of his time on the phone with his solicitor in London, working out the details of both a trust for Flynn and arrangements to take care of Alice's future.

There was a decent lunch crowd in the restaurant when he arrived, but he quickly spotted his brothers, Oliver, Brodie and Jensen, and his sister Amelia waiting at a large table near the back. A rush of love for his family rose to the surface, competing with his annoyance as he joined them. He was happy that his brothers and sister had found love in this small Texas town, but it wasn't easy having his close-knit family living an ocean away.

Amelia stood and greeted him with a fierce hug. "I'm so happy for you, Charles," she said in her soft voice. "Clementine is over-the-moon excited about having another cousin, although she wishes someone could provide her with a girl cousin." She arched an eyebrow at her three other brothers.

"Maybe Charles can go for a girl the next time around," Oliver said, shaking his head. "Or perhaps there's another little Fortune he has yet to discover."

"Oliver, stop," Jensen said, his tone reproving. "We agreed to hear Charles's side of the story."

"Whose side have you heard so far?" Charles asked, sinking into the chair between Jensen and Brodie. Amelia and Oliver sat on the opposite side of the table.

"Lucie's," Brodie said with a grin.

"She was supposed to keep the news a secret." Charles took a drink of water from the glass in front of him. "I thought she was an expert at secrets."

"Only her own," Amelia clarified.

A waitress approached their table, looking a bit dazed at the prospect of taking orders from so many British

Fortunes. She'd regained some of her composure by the time she got to Charles. "You're the royal one," she said, after he had ordered a burger and fries.

Charles pointed to Jensen. "He's the one they call 'sir.'"

The woman darted a brief glance at Jensen, then focused her attention back on Charles. "But you give the royal treatment, right?"

Charles cringed at having the embarrassing ad campaign mentioned in front of his siblings. The way the woman phrased the question made him sound like some sort of British stud for hire.

His brothers snickered. "Oh, he gives it all right," Brodie offered, laughing until Amelia swatted him on the arm.

The waitress smiled and scribbled something on the bottom of her order pad. "If you're in town for a spell and want some good ole Texas hospitality, give me a call." She ripped off a strip of paper and tucked it under the edge of the ketchup bottle in the middle of the table. "Don't have to be a royal to know how to have fun."

She turned from the table toward the kitchen, her hips swinging as she walked.

Oliver shook his head. "I forgot that sort of thing happens everywhere you go, Charles."

"It's disgusting," Amelia murmured.

Brodie grinned. "But a bit impressive."

Charles moved the ketchup bottle to cover the phone number. "I hate it."

"Since when?" Jensen asked.

Since Alice, Charles wanted to answer, even though he'd grown weary of his reputation and the attention that went along with it before that. But being with Alice had made it hit home how much he wanted something more from his life.

"Our Charlie Boy is a father now," Amelia said, when he didn't answer his brother's question. "That changes things."

"Has it, Charles?" Brodie asked.

"Flynn has changed everything," Charles said, absently running his hand through his hair. "But I'm still me and I'm damned scared of mucking up the whole thing."

His siblings greeted that pronouncement with silence.

"This is the part where you tell me I can do it," he muttered. "Words of encouragement and all that rot."

Oliver blew out a breath. "As in, hurrah, Charles, congratulations on getting a potential gold digger pregnant and saddling yourself with a lifetime of responsibility when you can barely remember to change your socks and underwear each day." As the oldest of Josephine's two boys from her first marriage, Oliver had always been protective of his brothers and sisters, and the blunt words stung. In truth, the dig at Charles's own character was easier to stomach than the implied insult to Alice.

"She's not a gold digger," he growled. "I won't hear you say a word against her, Oliver." He pointed a finger at each of them. "Not one word from any of you. Yes, the baby was a shock, but Alice is a wonderful mother and she's worked hard to support Flynn on her own. She hasn't asked me for anything."

"But you've offered," Brodie suggested.

"Of course I have," Charles snapped. "He's my son, she's his mother and I—" He broke off, unsure how to finish the sentence when he could barely wrap his own mind around his feelings for Alice and Flynn.

"You care about her," Amelia suggested in a gentle tone.

Charles took a deep breath. "I do."

The waitress brought their food at that moment and the table was silent as they were served.

"That changes things indeed," Jensen said, when the waitress was gone.

"Have you talked to Mum?" Amelia asked.

Charles almost choked on the french fry he'd popped into his mouth. "Bloody hell, no. And I don't want any of you to, either. I know what she'd say about all of this."

Amelia leaned forward. "She'd tell you to marry her." His three brothers nodded. "Perhaps that idea is worth considering," his sister added. The brothers shook their heads.

"That's a terrible idea," Brodie said around a bite of club sandwich. "You can't possibly marry her."

"Why not?" Amelia sounded offended on Alice's behalf.

"Because it gives her the power," Brodie said, as if the answer was obvious.

"Shall I tell Caitlyn you said that?" Amelia retorted.

Brodie blanched. "No way."

"You need to get custody of the baby." Oliver adjusted the cuffs of his expensively tailored shirt.

"Joint custody?" Jensen asked.

Oliver considered that for a moment. "Sole custody."

"Don't be daft," Charles snapped. "I would never try to take Flynn from Alice."

"Do you have a picture of him?" Amelia asked, clearly trying to diffuse some of the tension at the table. Charles loved his siblings, but he'd forgotten that they could each have strong and very differing opinions.

He wiped his hands on a napkin and pulled out the cell phone from his pocket. He clicked on his photo stream and passed the phone across the table.

"He's beautiful," Amelia said with a sigh as she scrolled through the pictures Charles had taken yesterday of Flynn.

"The girl is beautiful, too," Brodie added, looking over Amelia's shoulder. He glanced at Charles. "Not your usual type."

"You don't need to scroll through all of them," he said, reaching for the phone.

Jensen grabbed it first and studied the photos, his eyebrows raised. "This one looks like she actually has a brain inside that lovely head."

"Alice is smart, funny and kind, in addition to being beautiful." Charles sighed. "I highly doubt she'd want anything to do with me if it weren't for Flynn."

"You look happy with them," Amelia said, taking back the phone and holding it aloft for all the brothers to see. The picture had been taken at the mall's food court. Charles had been snapping pictures of Flynn, and a few of Alice when he could sneak them in. A woman at the table next to them had offered to take a photo of "the whole family." Both he and Alice had been embarrassed by the attention but had posed for the camera. Now that Amelia pointed it out, Charles saw that he looked not only happy but also relaxed in the photo, something utterly foreign to him in the past few years.

"Why are you wearing a baseball cap with a longhorn silhouette on it?" Oliver asked as he tipped the phone closer. "And why does it look like you're in a shopping mall?"

Charles grabbed the device and shoved it into his pocket. "I want to spend time with Alice and Flynn but can't take the chance of anyone recognizing me. She took me shopping for a more American wardrobe."

Jensen looked intrigued at this bit of information. "You mean this girl isn't trying to exploit her connection to you?"

"Not at all," Charles confirmed. "Alice is even more worried than I am that the tabloids will discover I'm Flynn's father. We want to have time to figure things out between the two of us before anything goes public."

"So why go out at all?" Brodie asked. "Can't you simply visit her at her home or have her to your hotel suite?"

Charles thought about being alone with Alice and sighed. "It's complicated."

"He wants to sleep with her," Oliver said with a laugh.

"No," the other three siblings said at once.

"It will mess with her head," Amelia exclaimed.

Brodie pointed a fry at him. "It will mess with *your* head."

Jensen nodded. "Whatever you do, don't sleep with her."

It was the one thing his brothers and sister all agreed on, making Charles smile. He had no plans to take Alice to bed again, except he couldn't seem to stop his longing to touch her. Maybe if they were together again, he could get it out of his system. No. Even he was smart enough to realize that once more with Alice wouldn't possibly be enough.

"Agreed," he said, meaning the word as he spoke it. "I'm going to take the next couple of weeks to get to know Alice and Flynn better and figure out how to make things work between us."

"But…" Amelia prompted.

"But I will not sleep with her," Charles added, and his siblings smiled.

Chapter Seven

Alice tried to focus on her computer screen Thursday morning but still felt like she was in a fog, despite three cups of tarry black swill from the office coffeemaker. Flynn had woken several times the previous night and she'd given up the hope of sleep around 4:00 a.m. It hadn't helped that anytime she closed her eyes, Charles's face popped into her mind.

He'd texted on his return from Horseback Hollow Monday afternoon, but she'd texted back that she and Flynn had plans and they could get together over the upcoming weekend. It was an outright lie, but she'd wanted time to shore up her defenses before she saw him again. Unfortunately, that could take a lifetime, and she knew Charles was losing patience with her.

He'd left two messages and texted several more times on Tuesday but she hadn't responded. She tried to convince herself that she was doing the right thing, that taking it slow would be better in the long run for all of them.

The truth was, she missed him. She missed the way he made her laugh and the fact that she could tease and flirt with him. She missed the way he looked at her like she was the only woman on the planet, one more reason he was dangerous to her heart. She'd seen enough photos and online videos of Charles to understand he gave every woman with him the same smoldering gaze.

Alice wasn't special, and the fact that he made her feel that way was something she was having trouble overcoming. So her plan to compartmentalize her relationship with him seemed like the best option.

"Are you ready for the marketing meeting?" Meredith peered over the top of the cubicle. "Oh, my. You look awful."

"Thanks," Alice said, and patted her palms against her cheeks, hoping to encourage a little color in her sallow, tired complexion. "I didn't get much sleep last night."

"I gather it wasn't Bonnie Lord Charlie keeping you awake until the wee hours."

She huffed out a laugh. "Hardly."

"Aren't you pitching the new international tourism campaign today?"

"Yes." Alice stood and straightened her dark gray suit jacket. She'd dressed up today to look the part of a seasoned tourism professional rather than a haggard new mom. She wore a tailored suit and a pair of patent-leather sling backs that she hoped would distract her bosses from the bags under her eyes. "I've been rehearsing since early this morning, but now I can't seem to finish a sentence without..." she paused as her mouth stretched open of its own accord "...yawning."

"You can do this," Meredith said, but her tone wasn't convincing.

Alice took a deep breath and one more fortifying gulp of coffee. "I can do this," she repeated, although she didn't sound any more certain than her friend.

She followed Meredith to the conference room at the end of the hall, holding her notes and handouts tight to hide the trembling in her fingers. Maybe she should have switched to decaf for that last cup of coffee. She desperately wanted her boss to green-light her idea for a new campaign. This was an opportunity to be seen as something more than a researcher and data cruncher for the tourism board. She knew she was good at her job, but she wanted a chance to prove she could handle her own campaign.

She plastered a smile on her face as she walked into the conference room, then ran smack into Meredith's back as her friend came to a sudden stop in the doorway. Alice peered around Meredith and her smile froze in place.

Charles sat in the chair next to Amanda Pearson, Alice's direct supervisor. Several other board members sat around the large table. There were two empty seats, one at the far end and one on the other side of Charles.

"Ladies, don't stand there gawking," Amanda said with an airy laugh. "I believe you both know Charles Fortune Chesterfield."

Meredith continued to stare until Alice poked her in the back. "Sit down, Mer," she said with a hiss.

"Did you know he was going to be here?" Meredith whispered.

Alice gave a sharp shake of her head. "No, but act normal. I don't want Amanda to guess anything."

Meredith moved forward. "Lord Charles," she said, giving an exaggerated curtsy.

He stood, pulling at the cuffs of his crisp white dress shirt. "Please call me Charles," he said, bestowing on Meredith his most charming smile. "I don't actually possess a title, despite what the tabloids would have you believe." He took Meredith's hand in his, and Alice could see her normally flirty friend's mouth drop open. Alice had started to think of the way women responded to him as "the Charles Effect."

Alice was determined to be immune to the Charles Effect today.

"It's nice to see you," Alice said, keeping her voice neutral. She took a step toward the far end of the table, but Charles held out the chair next to him.

"Please sit here, Ms. Meyers. I'm looking forward to hearing what you have to say this morning."

Meredith scooted to the empty chair at the end, leaving Alice to drop into the seat near Charles. Somehow she knew he was referring more to an explanation of why she'd blown him off the past few days than her campaign proposal.

"Charles is interested in working more with our office," Amanda explained, "and for whatever reason, Alice, he knows you from last year's conference." Her boss looked baffled as to why a man like Charles would remember Alice.

"It was your research," Charles said smoothly. "The figures you presented to support the impact of global tourism on the Texas economy were impressive."

He dropped his voice so low that only she could hear. "Everything about you impresses me, Alice."

Her gaze crashed into his for a second. That was all

the time she needed for the Charles Effect to kick in. Alice shook her head, trying to keep it clear.

"I thought it would be a good idea for Charles to attend this meeting, since he's in Austin for a few weeks." Amanda gave Alice a pointed look. "I hope he won't be disappointed."

"That seems unlikely," Charles added.

"Are you okay, Alice?" her boss asked. "You look pale."

"Fine." Alice wasn't sure she could say more than that at the moment. She was too busy trying not to react to Charles sitting so close to her. Her presentation and handouts were clenched in her fists, and she felt Charles lightly touch her wrist.

"Take a breath, Alice," he whispered. "You can do this."

She stood suddenly, wrenching her hand away from his. "The title of the campaign," she announced, clearing her throat when her voice came out in a squeak, "is It's Texas to Me, and while it fits into the larger scheme of the official state tourism campaign, it's also specific to the international market." She walked around the table as she spoke, placing a handout that showed a print ad mock-up in front of each person. "In our research we've discovered that a large percentage of first-time travelers to the United States from other parts of the world visit New York or California. Typically, they add Texas to the itinerary on subsequent trips, but we want to make the Lone Star State a first-run vacation destination."

She moved back to her place at the table but continued standing. It was easier to keep a bit of distance between herself and Charles this way. "The idea is that we'll showcase real people from other countries who have vacationed in the state and what Texas means to them. We'll show them with people from here—iconic cowboys, musicians, celebrities who call Texas home."

Several of the board bigwigs nodded as she made eye contact, bolstering her confidence. "We'll focus on what's special about each region, from the beaches of South Padre Island to the quaint shops of the hill country to the music scene in Austin. The goal is to give it a personal flavor and help travelers feel they have a connection to Texas before they even leave home. To make them think of Texas as their top-choice destination for an American vacation."

Amanda held up a hand before she could continue. "I think we've heard enough, Alice." The woman's smile was brittle and Alice realized she'd been right in suspecting that her boss hadn't really expected her to succeed. "That was—"

"Brilliant," Charles interrupted, quickly applauding. The rest of the attendees followed suit, and Amanda's smile froze in place.

"It was a good pitch," the woman allowed. "Perhaps I wouldn't go as far as brilliant."

"I agree with Charles," David McAvoy, the president of the tourism board, chimed in.

Alice felt her face flush as she sat down again. Charles gave her knee a friendly squeeze under the table. "I want to be involved," he told the group. "The ties I have to Texas have recently become more personal." He shot Alice a veiled glance. "And I can leverage my international contacts and the Fortune name here in the States to draw famous faces to the campaign. It has a universal enough appeal to be used in other countries, as well. I imagine the British Tourism Council might be keen on

an It's Britain to Me campaign to run here in the States."
He unleashed one of those killer smiles on Amanda. "If
you're willing to allow Alice to lend me her expertise."

"Of course," Amanda told him, and for a moment
Alice wondered if Charles was part vampire or some
other nonhuman creature, given his ability to dazzle everyone he met with just a dashing grin.

"I have a lunch across town," David announced, "but
get me a budget and time frame for the campaign by tomorrow morning, Alice. I'm going to put It's Texas to
Me on the fast track."

"Thank you, sir," Alice said quietly. She stared at
Charles while everyone else left the conference room.

"You surprised me today, Alice," Amanda said from
the doorway.

Alice met her boss's steely gaze. "I surprised myself."

"I hope you can handle everything managing a campaign involves."

"I will."

Amanda took a step forward. "I've been thinking
about a change in title for you, and this seems like the
right time. I'm going to move you from travel research
associate to tourism research manager."

Alice swallowed. "Thank you."

"Let's meet tomorrow morning to discuss new job
responsibilities and a salary bump."

"Sounds good, Amanda."

"Charles, do you have lunch plans?" Amanda asked,
running a hand through her thick hair. "I'd love to hear
your thoughts on some of our other upcoming cam-
paigns."

"Thanks for the lovely offer," Charles said smoothly,
stepping forward. "But I do. I'd like to get a few more

details on Alice's plan, but will stop by your office before I head out."

Her boss, who Alice knew had gone through a divorce late last year, wasn't deterred. "How long are you in town?"

"That depends," he answered.

"Give me a call," Amanda said in a soft purr Alice had never heard before. "I'd be happy to show you around Austin."

"I appreciate that. It's a marvelous city."

"They say everything's bigger in Texas." Amanda winked. "But there's plenty that's also better—like the women."

Charles chuckled, while Alice tried not to gag. Amanda was flirting with him as if Alice wasn't even in the room. And while the line was cheesy, she knew Charles probably heard a half dozen like it every time he left his hotel. It felt like every woman in the state was vying to be the next notch on Bonnie Lord Charlie's belt.

But not Alice. She was immune to the Charles Effect. Totally immune.

As Amanda left, Alice walked around the table, straightening chairs with a little more force than necessary. "Are you going to go out with my boss?"

"Of course not." Charles looked offended. "I'd like to go out with you if you'd ever return my messages and texts."

"I've been busy," she answered, gathering her notes from the table.

"You have a four-month-old baby."

"Who keeps me busy."

"Who goes to bed early each night," Charles countered.

"Me, too."

"A tempting thought," he said in a low whisper.

Alice closed her eyes and concentrated on stomping down the butterflies fluttering across her belly. "Why are you here, Charles?" she asked, when she felt safe looking at him again.

"For you," he answered, his gaze darkening.

And just like that, her defenses crumbled into a pitiful pile around her ankles.

She searched for a way to quickly rebuild them. "How was Horseback Hollow?"

"Have lunch with me."

"That didn't answer my question."

He grinned, but it was different than the one he'd given both Meredith and Amanda. This one seemed genuine, less practiced, as if her prickliness amused him. "Have lunch with me and I'll tell you all about it."

"You told Amanda you had plans."

"I do." He held out a hand. "With you."

"I haven't said yes. Maybe I already have a lunch date."

"Say yes, Alice."

She sucked in a breath and opened her mouth to refuse him. If she was going to have any chance of surviving the next eighteen years of her son's life, she had to set boundaries with Charles that wouldn't end with her heart being broken.

But he looked so hopeful waiting for her answer, as if he really wanted to be with her and not Amanda or Meredith or any other of his usual bevy of beautiful women. And despite what she tried to tell herself, Alice wanted to be with Charles more than was smart or safe.

She'd spent most of her life being prudent. The one

time she hadn't been, she'd ended up pregnant. But Flynn was the best thing that had happened to her, so maybe a bit of recklessness thrown into the mix wasn't so bad.

"We can't be seen walking out of the office together," she told him. "It would seem weird to everyone."

"Why?"

She shrugged. "Because men like you don't take women like me to lunch."

"This man does."

Her heart hammered in her chest. "Do you like Indian food?"

"I'm British," he said, as if that was an answer.

"What does that mean?"

"A real curry is almost as popular as fish and chips in London." He grinned again. "Yes, I like Indian."

"Good, because no one but me in this office does. There's a restaurant called Indian Palace around the corner from the building. You can order for both of us, and I'll meet you there in fifteen minutes."

His smile widened. "Cloak and dagger. I like it."

"Charles, be serious. You know we can't be seen together."

He nodded, but the smile remained. "If you really want privacy, my hotel is only a few blocks away."

"No hotel," she said, her voice coming out a squeak.

He laughed. "I'll see you in a bit, Alice." He stepped into her space before she could protest, traced his lips against her ear. "You really were brilliant today, love."

Alice's whole body heated and she grabbed hold of a chair to steady herself as she watched him disappear out of the conference room.

So much for guarding her heart against the sexy Brit.

* * *

Fatherhood was making him crazy. There was no other way for Charles to explain his actions today. He'd promised his siblings he had no intention of bedding Alice again, and he'd meant the words when he'd said them.

Then he'd proceeded to race back to Austin from Horseback Hollow with the hopes of spending more time with her. With Flynn, he corrected himself. He wanted to see his son. That was true, but not the whole truth. He'd missed both the boy and Alice during his short trip north to Horseback Hollow. The fact that Alice hadn't welcomed him back with open arms both irritated and intrigued him.

Women never avoided Charles. Never. Her reluctance to see him had made him only more intent on being with her. He'd tried to rationalize that he wanted to keep a friendly relationship with Alice for the sake of their baby, but that was ridiculous. He'd felt desperate to check in with her, to make sure he hadn't done something to cock up their tenuous bond.

Or maybe he just imagined a connection between them. Perhaps Alice wanted space to give him the subtle message that their relationship was simply two unattached parents working to raise their child. But he couldn't have forced himself to stay away from her even if he'd tried. From the moment she'd walked into that conference room, the anxious buzzing in his head had quieted and he'd felt an emotion strangely akin to contentment settle over him.

It had been impulsive to make a play for her at the tourism board office. He knew it was imperative they keep their ties to each other private, yet Charles couldn't resist the opportunity to see her, and working together would provide the most innocuous cover for doing so.

She walked into the restaurant at that moment, and all his doubts disappeared. She was as stunning in her business suit as she had been dressed for her role as mom, and Charles realized that he wanted to know more about every aspect of her life. Thanks to his famous family, his life was an open book. Now he wanted details about Alice and what made her tick.

He stood as she approached the booth he'd chosen in the far corner of the restaurant. A small smile played at the corner of her mouth, and he had the almost irresistible urge to brush his lips against hers again. But this wasn't her apartment or his hotel room, and while the half-empty restaurant appeared safe, he had to be careful whenever they were out together.

"Tell me about you," he said as she scooted into the booth across from him.

She seemed to stiffen under his regard. "There's not much to tell. Not everyone can be a jet-setting playboy."

He waved away the comment. "Old and boring news."

"No one thinks you're boring, Charles," she answered with a laugh. "Especially not women."

"There's only one woman I'm interested in, Alice."

She took a long sip of water. "You shouldn't say things like that."

"It's true."

She considered him for a moment. "I'm an Austin native. My father teaches American history at UT and my mom worked part-time as a teaching assistant at my elementary school."

"What were you like as a girl?" He leaned closer. "How will Flynn take after his mum?"

"He won't, I hope."

"You don't mean that. You're lovely, Alice. He'd be lucky to inherit your sweetness, not to mention your intelligence. Everyone on the board was blown away by you today."

She bit down on her lip as if his compliments made her uneasy. He started to ask her why, but the waiter brought the food.

"Chicken tikka masala, saag paneer and vindaloo," he said, placing the steaming dishes on the table. The young Indian waiter turned to the busboy who'd followed him to the table. "We also have basmati rice and naan for you to enjoy today."

"Thank you," Charles told the two men. "It looks delicious."

Alice's features relaxed as she looked at the food. "No one else I know likes Indian," she said, rubbing her palms together. "Sometimes I get it as takeout, but this is so much better."

Charles spooned a portion of each dish onto their plates and watched Alice take her first bite. Her eyes drifted closed, as if to better help her savor the taste, and she gave a soft moan.

"It's so good," she said with a sigh, her cheeks flushing when she opened her eyes to find him staring at her. "Silly to have that reaction to food, I know." She dabbed a napkin at the corner of her mouth.

"It's charming." Charles tore off a piece of naan, the bread warm between his fingers. "There is an amazing Indian place a couple of blocks from my flat in London. This is good…" He dipped the naan into the deep orange-red masala sauce. "But that restaurant takes it to a whole new level. We'll go there one day."

Her eyes widened, and the fork she held dropped to the table with a clatter.

"No pressure, Alice," he said quickly. "I know you want to take things slow."

She picked up the fork again and gave him a sheepish smile. "I don't even have a passport."

"You've never traveled abroad?"

"I've barely been out of Texas. My family went to California for a week when I was a girl because my dad had a conference there. And my grandparents retired to southern Colorado, so we'd drive to their cabin every summer. Otherwise…" She shrugged, as if apologizing. "You must think I'm a total country bumpkin. You're sophisticated and have traveled all over the world. I've been nowhere."

"You may live in Texas," Charles told her, reaching for her free hand, "but your taste in shoes definitely makes you more than a country girl."

She laughed at that and it made him enormously glad to be the man to put a smile on her face. "I do own cowboy boots," she told him.

"I can't wait to see them. Knowing you, they're something special." He laced her fingers with his. "I don't care that you haven't traveled." It was strangely appealing to think that he might be the one to introduce her to some of his favorite international destinations. Charles traveled so much for his work with the British Tourism Council, he'd become jaded, his senses dulled to the exotic locations and cosmopolitan cities. He wanted to see the world through Alice's eyes. "Where you've been doesn't matter to me. It's where we're going that counts."

"With Flynn," she said quickly, pulling her hand away.

"Of course," Charles agreed, tamping down the niggling sense of disappointment that curled through his gut. Alice was a fantastic mother, and he should be glad that their son was her first priority. Charles was, but it didn't stop him from wanting more. "When can I see him again?"

"He's usually tired and a little cranky in the evenings at the end of the workweek." She smiled. "Both of us are."

"I'll take tired and cranky," Charles told her. "From both of you."

She studied him for a moment, as if trying to determine if he really meant that. "I don't want to take him out tonight, but you could come over for dinner. Or stop by later if you have other plans."

"No other plans, and I'd love to come for dinner. I'll pick up a pizza. Everyone in America likes pizza, right?"

She laughed at that. "Not everyone, but most of us. A pizza would be great. Thank you."

"Two dates in one day." Charles saluted her with his water glass. "I'm a very lucky bloke."

Chapter Eight

Alice had just slipped into a pair of loose yoga pants when the doorbell rang. She glanced in the mirror and immediately regretted her decision to change from her suit into more comfortable clothes. At least dressed for work, she looked a bit put together. In her T-shirt and sweatpants she was the quintessential exhausted new mom. That couldn't be appealing to someone like Charles.

She pulled out the elastic band that held back her hair, letting her blond waves curl against her cheeks. Her hair might be a mess, but at least it falling in her face might camouflage her wan complexion.

The doorbell buzzed again, and she lifted Flynn from where he lay on her bed and went to answer it.

Unlike Alice, Charles looked totally put together, even in his casual jeans and T-shirt.

"Delivery," he said, holding up the cardboard pizza box.

She laughed and stepped back to let him into her apartment. "If all delivery guys looked like you, every single woman in America would be eating pizza seven nights a week."

"You have it all wrong, love. Tonight I'm a ubiquitous Austin pizza guy," he told her in an over-the-top American accent. "I like blending in." He leaned forward to press a gentle kiss on Flynn's forehead. "Hullo there, my wee man."

Alice caught a whiff of Charles's shampoo over the tangy scent of the pizza and bit back a groan. Inviting him to dinner had seemed like a good idea a few hours ago, but now she remembered why she'd insisted on spending time with him in public locations. Even as exhausted as she was, Charles made her body hum to life. The soft cotton T-shirt stretched across the muscles of his back and the jeans fit him in a way that made her mouth water.

"Shall I hold him?" he asked, setting the box on her coffee table.

Alice blinked, trying to gain control of her raging need. She wanted to beg Charles to hold *her*, wanted to press against all that strength and forget about her exhaustion and stress. She wanted to lose herself, and the unwanted thought that she was already losing her heart washed over her, an icy dose of reality.

"Sure," she said, careful not to let herself touch Charles as she deposited the baby in his arms. "I'll get plates. Would you like a beer or glass of wine?"

"Beer, please."

Charles balanced the baby in his arms, and Flynn rubbed at his eyes, letting out a tired cry.

"I'm sorry," Alice said automatically. "I know you probably don't want to deal with him fussy."

"I'm his father," Charles said, quirking a thick brow. "I'd venture to guess this isn't the worst I'm going to have to handle in the next few years."

Years. Alice gripped the pizza box tight in her hands. She'd have years to wallow in her unrequited lust for Charles. The only positive she could see was she'd save tons of money on hot water as she imagined many cold showers in her future.

She set two plates and napkins on the small table in her dining area, then grabbed a couple bottles of locally brewed beer from the refrigerator. "I can take him while you eat," she told Charles, opening the box he'd brought. The pizza was covered with fresh mozzarella, basil and tomatoes. Her stomach growled in response.

Charles chuckled. "I'll hold him while *you* eat." He bounced Flynn gently and the baby let out another cry, but slowly settled into the crook of Charles's arm with a yawn.

"He needs his last bottle before he falls asleep."

"I think I can manage a bottle."

"I'll make it," Alice offered, but Charles shook his head. "Tell me what to do."

She thought about arguing. Alice was so used to doing everything on her own that it was hard to delegate tasks related to Flynn.

"Alice, let me help." Charles's voice was low and coaxing.

She felt ridiculous tears prick the back of her eyes. She wanted to, but was afraid to depend on him, then be left on her own again. It was irrational and probably a result of being so tired. Sometimes she felt that if she actually stopped moving, working, struggling—even for a few minutes—she'd crumple under the weight of her life and never surface again.

But Charles was Flynn's father, and she'd sought him out. She owed him a chance to be a real part of her baby's life.

"There's a machine in the corner of the counter. Take a bottle from the cabinet above and put it under the spout like a coffeemaker. Hit the red button and the formula and heated water will mix. Just make sure you screw the cap on tight before feeding him." She smiled. "I made that mistake once and ended up with formula all over both of us."

"Got it." Charles held out a chair. "Sit down, Alice. Enjoy a beer and a slice of pizza. I'll take care of Flynn." He winked at her. "You can supervise."

"Supervise," she murmured, dropping into the chair. "I'll work on that." She bit into a piece of pizza, amazed at how much better it tasted when she could actually take a moment to enjoy it. These days she scarfed down most of her meals while caring for Flynn, or at her desk at lunch so she wouldn't be late picking him up from the sitter's. Two meals in one day with Charles, and she'd felt pampered at both of them. It was embarrassing how easily she could get used to the sensation.

"This is like an espresso machine for formula," Charles said as the machine whirred.

"It was a splurge," Alice admitted. "I used some of the gift cards I'd gotten for his shower. With his night-time sleeping patterns, it's made things much easier."

"I'm all for easier," Charles said as he balanced Flynn in one arm and tightened the cap. He sat in the chair across from her and tipped the bottle into Flynn's mouth.

The baby's eyes drifted closed even as he gulped down the formula. "It's like he's asleep but still eating." Charles smiled at Flynn. "An impressive lad, indeed."

"I'm going to start him on cereal this weekend," Alice said, taking a sip of beer. "If you want to be here…"

"I wouldn't miss it."

Alice watched the two most important men in her life for a few minutes. There was a quiet intimacy to the three of them sitting in her small apartment, Flynn's contented gurgling as he ate the only sound. She wished it could be like this all the time, then mentally kicked herself for entertaining the thought. They weren't a family, and pretending they were would only lead to heartbreak. "I can take him now, if you want pizza before it gets cold."

"I'm fine," Charles told her, still looking at Flynn. "I can't get over having a mini me running around in the world."

"Being carried and pushed by stroller through the world, you mean."

"He'll be running soon enough." Charles shot Alice an apologetic glance. "If Flynn is anything like me, he'll keep you on your toes. My mum was constantly having to bail me out of scrapes and misadventures when I was a boy. She said I had enough energy for twins."

"Good to know." Alice huffed out a laugh and took another drink of beer. "I bet you got away with a ton because you were too cute to stay mad at for long."

Charles grinned. "It still works that way."

Flynn had finished the bottle and was now dozing in Charles's arms. Lucky baby. "I'm stuffed." Alice stood and placed her plate in the sink. "I'll change him and put him down for the night." She took the baby from Charles. "Thank you for the help and for dinner."

"My pleasure on both counts."

She put Flynn into a fresh diaper and his pajamas and then settled him in his crib. He snuggled against the soft sheet with a sleepy sigh. Alice stifled a yawn. Flynn always went down without a fuss, although staying asleep for the night was a bigger challenge.

By the time she returned to the kitchen, Charles had loaded the dishwasher, put the leftover pizza in the refrigerator and was wiping the table.

"Are you always this perfect?" she asked, leaning against the door frame.

"Hardly ever," he said with a grin. "You seem to bring out the best in me." He hung the dishrag over the faucet and turned.

They watched each other for several moments, awareness ricocheting through the small space. Charles crossed his arms over his chest, the muscles of his arms bunching in a way that made Alice want to...

Nope. Not going there.

"I should probably go," he said, but didn't make a move to leave.

"Do you want to watch a movie?"

One side of his mouth curved. "Can you stay awake for a whole movie?"

"How about a TV show?" she amended. "Not that you have to stay. I guess with Flynn asleep there's no reason..."

"I'd love to stay." Charles crossed the room to her, tucking a lock of her hair behind her ear with one finger. "Would you believe in all my travels to the States, I've never watched American television other than in an airport waiting area?"

She rolled her eyes. "Because you normally have way more exciting things to do."

"Nothing excites me more than you, Alice." His voice was pitched low and that familiar melting sensation started in her belly. His head moved closer, just inches, but Alice felt his breath tease her cheek. She waited for the touch of his mouth on hers, but instead he straightened. "Well, then," he said, clearing his throat. "What's on the programming menu tonight?"

"Reality TV or crime dramas." She forced herself to take a step back so she wouldn't be tempted to plaster herself to the front of him.

"You're not planning to subject me to any type of housewives?"

She laughed and they moved toward the overstuffed couch in her family room. "How do you feel about surviving the Alaskan wilderness?"

"Better to watch than experience it firsthand."

She turned on the lamp that sat on the end table next to the sofa, then grabbed the remote. "Let your introduction to the other side of American culture begin."

Charles had to admit he found the program about life on the frozen Alaska tundra fascinating. But it wasn't half as riveting as the beautiful woman curled up next to him. Alice had fallen asleep before the first commercial break, but Charles hadn't woken her.

He knew if he did, she'd be embarrassed and apologetic and most likely make him leave. The last thing he wanted was to return to his luxurious hotel room. In truth, the only thing he wanted was to stay in this tiny, simple apartment with Alice tucked in the crook of his arm. For all the years he'd spent partying and traveling, his old lifestyle held no appeal now.

He felt useful with Alice, needed in a way that filled his soul. It had always seemed like a sign of weakness that even in a crowd of fun, fancy people he could feel so alone. But now he understood it was the connection to another person he'd been missing. The motivation to be something more than anyone expected.

The monitor that sat on the coffee table crackled and Flynn gave a small cry. Alice stirred, made a sweet, snuffling noise, then snuggled closer to him. As gently as he could, Charles turned down the volume on the monitor and rearranged Alice so her head was on a pillow instead of his shoulder.

Nerves danced across his skin as he quietly walked into the baby's bedroom and flipped on the low-wattage lamp on the dresser. It was ridiculous to be nervous at the thought of going in alone to his son, but until now all his interactions with Flynn had been under Alice's watchful eye. That's how Charles had wanted it. The easy way. A week of being a father and he could already feel himself falling into the pattern of popping in when it suited him, armed with toys or goodies, but disappearing again if there was real parenting work to be done.

It made sense to leave that to Alice. She was far more comfortable in her role as mother than he feared he'd ever be as a dad.

But he wanted to try.

He approached the crib as if Flynn might pop up, jack-in-the-box style, at any second. Another silly thought, since the baby couldn't even sit up on his own yet. As Charles peered over the crib railing, Flynn lay on his back, staring up at him even as he continued to cry.

"What's wrong, little man?" Charles reached out a hand and placed it on the baby's rounded belly. Flynn took a few shuddered gulps of air and opened his mouth, seemingly poised to let out a true wail. Not wanting to wake Alice, Charles gathered the boy into his arms and started bouncing. The baby's cry cut off and he reached out, poking his fingers at Charles's face.

"See now," Charles crooned. "Everything's fine. Did you have a bad dream or—" He broke off as the smell of something rotten hit his nose. It was putrid and rank, making Charles want to gag. Flynn smiled, then squirmed in his arms. Charles could imagine whatever it was in that diaper being ground into the baby's soft bottom. Even he knew that wasn't good.

He'd never come close to changing a diaper. Not for his niece or his nephews. Hell, nappies were as foreign to him as braiding hair. He glanced at the door to the family room and thought about fetching Alice. As with most things related to Flynn, dirty diapers were her area of expertise.

So much for Charles's valiant effort at parenting through thick and thin. He'd meant "thick" in a hypothetical way, not scraping a baby's bottom.

Then he looked again at Flynn blinking up at him, lashes wet with glistening tears. The boy shoved his fist in his mouth and loudly sucked, observing Charles with a thoughtful stare as if measuring his worth as a father.

Charles did *not* want to be found lacking.

"We can manage this," he said out loud—to himself as much as Flynn. The changing table was situated next to the crib and seemed equipped to handle a veritable army of baby bums. A stack of diapers were arranged in a basket on the shelf under the changing pad, along with a container of wipes, several tubes of lotion and cream, and a toy that looked like a psychedelic bumblebee.

He lay Flynn on his back on the pad and connected the straps that hung on either side across the baby's belly. "First things first," Charles whispered, and handed him the bee to play with. Next he grabbed the wipes and a diaper, then began unsnapping the footed pajamas the baby wore. As soon as Charles opened the front of the sleeper, another wave of nasty nappy stench hit him. He realized he probably should have turned on the overhead light so he could actually see what he was doing. At the same time, he didn't really want to see in too much detail.

"You must be a chip off the old block," he told Flynn, "because you've certainly made a royal mess." Although the room was cool, Charles felt sweat drip down the side of his face. He wiped it on his shoulder, then took a deep breath, holding it as he undid the diaper and opened it.

"Bloody hell." He blinked, cringed and began grabbing handfuls of wipes to clean up the mess. Flynn patiently gummed his toy and then kicked his legs.

"Stop," Charles yelled, before he thought better of it. Flynn's rosebud mouth turned down in a pout. "Sorry, chap," Charles said, forcing his voice to be cheerful. "But you don't want to step in it when we've almost got you cleaned up."

Unfortunately, the *almost* seemed to last far longer than it should. Charles wiped and wiped but couldn't seem to remove all the mess. "How does your mum do this every day?" he asked the boy.

"Believe it or not, it gets easier with practice."

Charles glanced behind him to see Alice coming through the door.

"I didn't want to wake you," he said.

"You didn't." She nudged him to the side. "Mind if I take over?"

"Please," he muttered. "I'm utter rot with nappies."

"You're trying," she said, and gave him a sleepy smile. "I woke up and the monitor wasn't on, so I came looking for the two of you."

"Flynn had a postdinner explosion."

"He's not crying." Alice deftly finished the job of cleaning the baby and putting on a new diaper. She placed the dirty one and all the wipes into a garbage can next to the changing table. The diaper pail whirred when she snapped the lid shut.

"I hope that thing's rated for hazardous materials," Charles commented.

"I've heard it gets worse when he starts solid foods." She rearranged the sleeper, pried the toy out of Flynn's hands and picked him up off the pad. "Did you give your daddy a big mess to handle?" she cooed to the baby, snuggling him close.

Daddy. Charles preened at the word. Okay, maybe he hadn't handled the diaper change like a pro, but he tried his best. As a daddy would.

"Do you want to put him down again?" she asked, smiling up at Charles.

"Sure." He took the baby from her, Flynn burrowing against his chest. "Your mum needs a break, little man. How about you stay asleep until morning?"

Flynn didn't answer, but he also wasn't crying in protest, which Charles took as a win. He leaned over the crib and placed him on the sheet. The baby kicked and swatted at the air, but almost immediately his eyes drifted shut. "Good night, little one," Charles whispered.

Alice was watching them from where she stood near

the dresser. She flipped off the light and Charles followed her to the kitchen sink.

"You did good in there," she said as she turned on the faucet and handed him the soap.

"I've never seen anything like that," he said with a small shudder.

"Like you said, he's an *impressive lad*."

Charles laughed at the way she mimicked his accent and they finished washing hands in a companionable silence.

"I'm sorry I fell asleep," she said as she led him back into the family room. "This must be the most boring night you've had in years."

"Hardly," he said, tapping one finger to the tip of her nose. "Boring is being stuffed into an uncomfortable monkey suit in a room full of pompous strangers, counting the minutes until you can make a polite exit."

"Right." Alice made a face. "Sipping expensive champagne and surrounded by beautiful women. You're not fooling me, Charles."

"Sincerity isn't one of my best traits," he admitted, "but I mean every word of it. I can think of no place I'd rather be than here with you and our baby."

She stilled at his final words. *Our baby*. He wondered if she regretted inviting him into her life. There was no doubt she wanted him to have a relationship with Flynn, but Alice was the first woman in his life he couldn't seem to read. The only woman who'd ever really mattered romantically.

He forced himself to take a step away from her, to give her the space he guessed she needed. "I should let you get to bed, too."

Something in her hazel eyes flashed. "Because I'm a tired wreck?"

He pushed his hands into the front pockets of his jeans. "Because I'm trying to be a gentleman here."

She stared at him for another minute, then tugged her bottom lip into her mouth. Desire shot through him like a cannon and he took another step toward the door. He was about to turn and grab the handle when Alice closed the distance between them and pressed a gentle kiss to the corner of his mouth.

So much for being a gentleman.

Chapter Nine

Alice didn't want Charles to be a gentleman, and she wasn't about to let him leave without kissing him. She knew it was reckless, but she couldn't manage one more second without being close to him again.

The need had been building inside her all night, despite her exhaustion. Who could blame her? Charles was a fantasy for women around the world. But it was watching him fumble in the dim light of Flynn's nursery that had pushed her over the edge. There was nothing more important to her than her son, and for Charles to be making an effort to truly support her as a father was about the sexiest thing she'd ever seen—even if he had no idea what he was doing.

He tasted as amazing as she remembered, spicy, refined and just a touch exotic. He could wear American clothes all day long, but he was British upper class to his core. More importantly, he was a man.

Right now he was hers.

He gathered her into his arms and framed her face with his hands. His kisses were gentle and slow, like he was savoring her. Although inexperienced, Alice had always thought of a kiss as a prelude to what came after. But Charles pressed his mouth to hers like this was the main event. He was in no hurry to race to the next stop. His tongue traced the seam of her lips, coaxing them open, and she felt her knees give way. Talk about melting.

Without breaking the kiss, Charles turned, pressing Alice's back to the door as he deepened the kiss. His fingers trailed through her hair and as his kisses grew hotter and more demanding, Alice heard herself moan. That small sound seemed to spur him on and he circled her hips with his hands, pulling her hard against him.

"Charles," she whispered, her body tingling from head to toe, "I want..." She didn't quite know how to ask for what she wanted from him, but in the end it didn't matter.

Her voice seemed to yank him out of the moment. He pushed away from her, leaving Alice sagging against the door, her breath coming out in strangled gasps.

"I'm sorry, Alice," he said, his own voice strained.

"Don't—"

He held up a hand. "That shouldn't have happened. I can't..." He ran a hand through his hair, met her gaze with a crooked smile. "You're a lovely girl, but we can't go there." His tone had gentled, and Alice couldn't help but think she wasn't the first woman to be brushed off with that soothing accent.

"Why?"

He blinked at her direct question, and even Alice was

surprised at her own bluntness. Apparently sexual frustration made her bold.

"Well…" His blue eyes roamed over her. "It would complicate things between us."

Alice laughed, pressing the back of her hand to her kiss-swollen lips. "Because they're so simple now?"

His smile faltered. "Sleeping together would muddy the waters. I need to… We need to keep our focus on the baby."

Alice understood the sentiment, but it felt like a rejection nonetheless. Maybe Charles hadn't enjoyed kissing her the way she had him. Her desire felt one-sided, a little pathetic and a whole lot embarrassing.

She grabbed for the handle of the door, stepping back as it opened. "I understand," she whispered. "Good night, Charles."

"Alice—"

"Good night," she said again, more firmly. She forced herself to meet his gaze, to prove to him she wasn't breaking apart inside.

He lifted his hand but she gave a sharp shake of her head. "Don't. Please."

He looked as miserable as she felt. "I'll call you tomorrow."

She wanted to tell him no, to cut Charles out of her life for good. But he was the father of her son, and she would do right by Flynn no matter what.

"Tomorrow," she agreed, and shut the door behind him.

But Charles didn't call the next day. Instead he showed up for her late-morning meeting to finalize dates on the new campaign. Looking at him in his tailored suit and crisp white dress shirt, his hair still damp at the ends, made Alice's lungs stop working for a second. She tapped her chest with her knuckles, reminding her body to do its job and her lungs to keep pumping air in and out.

He was attentive and charming to all the women from the research and marketing departments in the conference room. More importantly, he was respectful of Alice and her ideas about It's Texas to Me. It was difficult to hold on to her anger in the face of his overt kindness. It was almost as if he was trying to make up for what he wouldn't give her last night. Even if he wasn't attracted to her, she knew Charles genuinely cared for her as Flynn's mother. Somehow that would have to be enough.

Of course, it wouldn't be easy to spend the rest of her life comparing herself to the type of woman who would interest Charles. He was seated next to her boss. Amanda, flipping her shiny blond hair and decked out in a bright red power suit that showed off her curvy figure, fawned over him and made a show of inviting him to lunch after the meeting. Alice tried not to pay attention until she realized Charles had declined Amanda's offer and was turning to her.

"We're still on for lunch?" he asked.

Alice felt her mouth drop open and quickly snapped it shut.

"Remember, we'd planned to discuss my ideas for tweaking the campaign to make it appropriate for several of the countries involved with the European Tourism Board, and how I could help with my contacts."

"Sure," Alice stammered, and glanced at her boss, who was glaring at her from the far end of the table. "I hope you don't mind."

"Of course she doesn't," Charles said, before Amanda

could answer. He flashed her a brilliant smile and took Amanda's hand, brushing the barest kiss across her knuckles. "You understand, love?"

"Of course," Amanda agreed with a giggle. Alice rolled her eyes. Cue the Charles Effect.

Meredith leaned close to Alice's ear as she stood from the table. "He wants you bad."

"We have a child together," Alice whispered. "That's all there is between us."

Meredith gave her a funny look but didn't argue.

Alice grabbed her purse from her cubicle and went to find Charles. He was waiting for her in the lobby, the tourism board's longtime receptionist watching him as he stared out the window.

"The phones are ringing," Alice said, tapping on the desk as she walked by.

The receptionist jumped, then threw Alice a cagey smile. "How anyone in England gets work done when that man is around is beyond me."

He turned as Alice approached and she had to agree with the other woman's assessment.

Charles smiled, almost tentatively, and took a step toward her. "About last night," he began, but Alice shook her head.

"I don't want to talk about it, and especially not here." She glanced over her shoulder to where two other women from the office had gathered at the receptionist's desk. Charles was like some rare object on display—the elusive British bachelor. Right now, she wasn't in the mood to entertain a group of prying eyes. "Let's go." She grabbed his arm and dragged him out the door.

The noonday sun was almost violently bright, and she shoved her sunglasses onto her nose. "What are you doing showing up at my office again?" She started down the busy sidewalk, releasing Charles as they jostled through the crowd. But when she turned to look at him, he was gone, only to pop up again on her other side.

At her questioning gaze, he shrugged. "A gentleman always walks on the street side when with a lady."

"In case she wants to shove him into traffic?"

He smiled. "Among other reasons."

"Is that a British thing?"

"I'm not sure. It's something my father taught us." He looked down at her as they stopped at a crosswalk. "I'll teach Flynn one day."

An immediate tingle coursed through her. The ladies at her work might be susceptible to the Charles Effect, but her feelings for him were far more dangerous. "You didn't answer my question."

"I came to talk about the campaign," he said, placing his fingers on her elbow as the light changed and she stepped off the curb. "Plus I wanted a chance to spend time with you and not feel it necessary to hide out."

"Why?" she couldn't help but ask. "I assumed you said everything you needed to last night."

"Hardly. I want to be your friend, Alice. The connection we share is powerful."

She drew in a shaky breath at his words, even as she understood he was talking about their baby. "Based on what I've seen in the papers, you have plenty of friends."

"Acquaintances," he clarified. "Not the same thing at all."

She had to hide her smile at the knowledge that this dashing man had chosen her. Even if she wanted more, she had to find a way to be satisfied with friendship.

He glanced around as she guided him toward another intersection. "Where are you taking me?"

"The best lunch place in Austin," she said with a grin.

"You like food," he observed, and she glanced up at him again. He wasn't wearing sunglasses and his eyes were almost the same color as the spring sky.

"Last time I checked, eating is pretty essential to a person's survival."

He pushed her hair off her forehead with the tips of his fingers. "It wasn't an insult, Alice. But I'm used to women who are more concerned with moving the food around on their plates than with actually taking a bite."

"I bet they eat a lot of salad, too."

He nodded. "Most seem partial to lettuce, yes."

She couldn't help but laugh. "Maybe the lifestyle of the rich and famous isn't all it's cracked up to be." She led him down a path that intersected the sidewalk near the park's entrance. "Because I'm about to blow your mind, Mr. Fortune Chesterfield."

Chapter Ten

Charles wanted to tell Alice she'd already blown his mind on so many levels. It went way beyond making him a father, as shocking as that revelation had been. Alice seemed unimpressed with his reputation and the trappings of his fame, a wholly unfamiliar experience for Charles but one he'd quickly grown to appreciate.

Case in point was that they now stood in front of a brightly painted recreational vehicle, a new Texas experience for Charles. He was used to dining at steak houses and trendy bistros, but took his place in the short queue behind Alice.

"A food truck?"

"The best tacos in Austin." She pointed to the large chalkboard hanging from the side of the truck. "They have daily specials, but my favorite is the Chicken Sink."

"Is that supposed to sound appetizing?" He cocked a brow, earning a laugh.

"It's a chicken taco with everything but the kitchen sink thrown in."

"I'm sure there is an American cultural reference I'm missing, but…"

Her grin widened. "It means there's a ton of stuff on top of the chicken." She held up her hand, ticking off ingredients with her fingers. "Guacamole, green chili, sour cream and *queso*, plus salsa and a bit of shredded lettuce. They don't use a ton of any one item, but you get a mix of all the different flavors."

"It's delish," the woman standing in front of them said, looking over her shoulder. Her gaze caught and held on Charles. "Wow," she murmured, then threw an apologetic glance at Alice.

"No worries," Alice told her. "Happens all the time. Eventually you get used to him."

"I'll take your word for it," the woman answered, and turned back around.

"What happens all the time?" Charles didn't begin to understand the exchange between the two women, but was quite curious.

"The Charles Effect," Alice said, before a blush rose to her cheeks. It was as if she hadn't meant to share those words with him. The line shifted and one of the servers beckoned them forward. "Saved by the taco," she muttered, before turning to Charles. "Do you know what you want?"

"What is the Charles Effect?" he asked.

"I'll order for both us." She ignored his question and requested a sampling of menu items from the clearly popular food truck. Charles handed the man a few bills before Alice could pull her wallet from her purse. "I dragged you halfway across downtown in the midday heat," she protested. "I can pay."

"Call me old-fashioned," he drawled.

As they shifted to the side to wait, Alice began to babble about the vast array of food trucks that could be found throughout Austin's various neighborhoods. "That should be one of our features for the ad campaign. Food is a big draw for vacationers, and my research shows that almost half will drive up to thirty miles from their intended destination to try a popular restaurant." She paused to catch her breath, then started to speak again, but Charles held a finger over her lips.

"Explain the Charles Effect."

"It's...you know...how women react to you."

"You mean the fact that women like me."

She barked out an indelicate laugh. "They more than *like* you, Charles. You mesmerize them."

"But not you?"

The man at the food truck called her name and she hurried forward to grab the paper sack. "There's a hidden park bench around the corner near the fountain. It's usually empty."

"Are you going to answer my question?" Charles asked as he followed her.

She kept her attention on the food, divvying up the foil-wrapped tacos after taking a seat on the bench. "Our friendship gives me immunity to your charm."

"Is that so?"

"Yep." She peeled back one corner of the foil and took a small bite of taco. "You need to eat. I only have an hour for lunch."

"Your boss won't mind if you're with me."

"David might not, but Amanda certainly will." Alice

dabbed a napkin at the corner of her mouth. "She wants you for herself."

"She can't have me." Charles bit into the taco and nodded. Both the food and his lunch companion made him happy. He was happier spending time with Alice than he could remember being in ages. "I like this kitchen sink."

"I told you," she said with another quick smile. "Do you have food trucks in London?"

"We do. You see them most often at festivals or in open-air markets. You need to get a passport, Alice. There's so much to see in the world."

She shrugged. "I've got a job and a baby. That doesn't leave much time for traveling."

"Or dating?"

She coughed wildly, and Charles thumped her on the back.

"That came out of nowhere," she said, as her breath returned to normal.

"We talk a lot about my social life, but I've heard almost nothing of yours."

"There isn't anything to share," she answered.

"So no dates since…" He trailed off.

She blushed again as those hazel eyes darkened to a deep green color. "Nope. No time. No inclination. No… just no."

"Are you really immune to me, Alice?"

"I am."

He leaned closer. "Could I change your mind?" His tone had gone low and silky, like the luxurious sheets she remembered from her one night in his hotel room.

"You won't try." She jumped up from the bench, walked to a nearby trash can and threw away the taco wrapper before turning back to him. "You were the one who said we could only be friends, Charles. I don't care how much you trifle with other people. You care about Flynn, and you aren't going to do anything that will mess this up." She walked back slowly, watching the emotions play across his face. "I trust you. I believe you'll do the right thing by your son."

She wished the right thing for both of them was being together, but Charles had already made his thoughts on the subject clear. The only reason he was toying with her now was because she posed a challenge. Even though he acted the part of the irresponsible rake, she knew he wouldn't willingly hurt Flynn.

"Damn," he muttered. "You certainly know how to set a high bar." He stuffed the rest of his uneaten taco into the bag and wiped a sleeve across his forehead. For the first time since she'd met him, Charles didn't look cool and in control. He seemed almost panicked at the idea of someone having expectations of him that didn't involve a drink and a laugh.

"There's an outdoor concert tonight at Zilker Park, on the lawn in front of the botanical garden." She sank down on the bench and nudged him with her elbow. "I'm going to take Flynn. It would be good to have a *friend* to go with us."

"Certainly," he said without hesitation, but Alice wasn't even sure he'd heard the invitation.

"We'll figure this out," she told him, resting her head on his wide shoulder. "Team Fortune Chesterfield and all that."

"Team Fortune Chesterfield," he repeated, and wrapped an arm around her waist.

They sat there for a few more minutes and she felt Charles slowly relax. Alice kept her breathing normal, even as awareness skittered across her skin and through her body. She tried to ignore it as best she could. Sexual frustration notwithstanding, it was nice to have a friend. If nothing else, Charles was her partner in parenting. It gave Alice more comfort than she cared to admit that she was no longer alone.

"I need to go," she said eventually, hating to break the connection between them. She lifted her head and Charles stood.

"We haven't discussed the campaign." He held out a hand to her and she slipped her fingers into his.

"Let's talk on the way back to the office."

He nodded but didn't let go of her hand. He threw away the rest of the trash from lunch, and she led him out of the park. Despite the necessity of it, she wasn't ready to return to her office and he didn't appear in a hurry to let her go. They talked about the campaign and he asked for a list of her favorite things in Austin. He seemed truly interested in what made it Texas to her. She started to rattle off the typical list of live music, food and the ubiquitous Western spirit, then changed her mind. Alice had always been more interested in the parts of Austin that could best be described as hidden gems.

She told him about the local graffiti park, the natural swimming hole at the Hamilton Pool Preserve and a few museums and galleries that weren't on most tourist itineraries. "Does that make me seem weird?" she asked, after promising to take him to one of the quaint neighborhoods she liked outside of town. "My job is all about the things that make Texas popular, but those aren't my favorite spots."

"On the contrary," he answered, taking her elbow as they crossed a busy intersection. "It's something we have in common. The places in London I prefer are the ones I can go to without fanfare—a bookstore tucked down a cobblestone street across from the British Museum in Bloomsbury, or a family-owned Italian restaurant on the outskirts of the theater district. I'd like to explore the places in Austin that appeal to you, Alice." Goose bumps rose on her skin at the way he said her name. "I want to discover them with you as my guide."

She forced herself to keep walking, when she wanted to stop and kiss him in the middle of the crowded street. It was disconcerting to find they shared this penchant for the unique. Charles was a man she could so easily love. What had started as a one-night stand had turned into much more.

But he'd offered her friendship, and that had to be enough.

Too soon they were at the entrance of the tourism board office. "I'm terrified of the woman who answers the phones," he said, glancing past Alice into the plated glass door. "She looks at me like she wants me for her next meal."

"I'd think you would be used to that look from women by now," Alice said with a laugh.

"Yes, but she looks hungrier than most."

Alice shook her head and laughed again. "I'll see you tonight, Charles."

He nodded and started to walk away, then turned back. "Until tonight, love," he said, and dropped a light kiss against her hair. The implied intimacy of the gesture made her heart squeeze.

She was quickly discovering that regular life was more exhilarating than she could have imagined with this man at her side.

* * *

Alice pushed Flynn's stroller through the crowd gathered in Zilker Park later that evening. She'd texted Charles to meet her on the lawn in front of the botanical garden, knowing it would be easier to walk than to deal with traffic and parking before the popular concert series.

Flynn made a noise and she pushed down his shade cover, not paying much attention to the people she passed on the sidewalk until a man stepped in front of her, blocking the path.

"Excuse me," she said, then glanced up into a pair of familiar blue eyes. "Charles, it's you."

"I take it my disguise is working," he said with a laugh, and bent forward to kiss Flynn's downy hair.

"You look like a Texan," she admitted as he fell in step beside her, "but the accent gives you away."

"Then I'll have to work on being the 'strong silent type.' I can channel my inner John Wayne."

Alice hid her smile. He definitely had the strong part down, with his broad shoulders and long-limbed gait. Although Charles wasn't dressed in his usual dapper British garb, her body still reacted to him. His fingers brushed hers as he took over handling the stroller, and warmth and desire spiked through her. He'd changed into a faded pair of jeans and an orange Texas Longhorns T-shirt, quintessential Austin fashion for a man in his late twenties. He wore a dark blue baseball cap and the work boots he'd bought when they were together.

"How did you break in those boots so quickly?" she asked, pointing to the scuffed toes.

"Would you believe I did some work on my brother-in-law's ranch?"

"Not for a second."

"You know me too well, Alice Meyers." He ruffled her hair. "The truth is, I gave them to the concierge at the hotel. His son is my size and works in construction." Charles laughed when she gaped at him. "Turns out the Four Seasons really is full-service," he said.

"Only you, Charles." She waved her hand toward an area near the top of the hillside. "Is that spot okay? It's far enough away from the stage to be safe for Flynn's ears. Plus he won't bother anyone if he gets fussy." She glanced around the crowded lawn. "Although there's not much shade on the hill. Maybe we could—"

"How about there?" Charles pointed to a clump of trees about halfway up the hill. Under the shade of the branches were two lawn chairs, with a blanket spread across the grass in front of them. A wicker picnic basket sat to one side with a galvanized-steel bucket next to it.

Her mouth dropped open. "Did the hotel take care of that, too?"

He shook his head. "I had some time on my hands this afternoon and wanted you and the baby to have a good spot for the concert."

"I don't know what to say... Thank you."

"I believe in full service, too."

She let him lead her to the picnic area, feeling like the luckiest woman on the planet. Well, she'd feel even luckier if this was a real date. How was any man going to measure up to Charles?

She brushed away the thought, rationalizing that she'd be too busy raising her son to worry about a man in her life.

She lifted Flynn from the stroller and set him on the soft

blanket. His gaze immediately caught on the leaves fluttering above him and he seemed as content as Alice felt.

"We have a selection of sparkling water or lemonade for the evening," Charles told her, making a comically gallant gesture toward the ice bucket.

"Lemonade, please," she said as she sat next to Flynn. Charles handed her a cold bottle, then lowered himself to the blanket on the other side of the baby. He pulled the picnic basket closer and took out a plate of cheeses and a box of gourmet crackers.

"This is perfect," Alice said with a sigh, stretching her legs in front of her. She saw a few people glance their way, but no one seemed to recognize Charles.

"To a perfect night," he agreed, and held up his can of sparkling water for a toast. They shared the cheese and crackers as the sun dipped behind the trees. Despite her awareness of him, Alice found it remarkably easy to talk to Charles. He asked her more questions about her childhood and shared stories of his brothers and sisters growing up in England.

As an only child with very little extended family, Alice loved the thought that her son would grow up knowing aunts, uncles and cousins. Of course, that thought was immediately followed by the worry that Charles would want to take Flynn off to either Horseback Hollow, or worse, England, and Alice would be left alone and missing her boy.

She was afraid to broach the subject and ruin the mood of this lovely evening. Charles had told her over lunch earlier that his family solicitor was finishing up the papers that would ensure Flynn was provided for, so Alice decided she could wait to talk about custody as part of that discussion.

Despite the noise around them, Flynn drifted off to sleep. Alice pulled a blanket from the bottom of the stroller and covered the baby.

As she glanced up at Charles she found him staring at her shoes. At first glance, these were relatively simple tan pumps. But the inside edge of the shoe was a band of lace, with corresponding lace panels on either side of her heel. They were demure but at the same time gave a glimpse of skin that made Alice feel quite sexy. It was no accident she'd chosen them for her evening with Charles. She might have agreed to be his friend, but that didn't mean she wouldn't tempt him when she could.

She stretched her foot forward, pointing her toe.

"More remarkable shoes," he murmured, shifting down the blanket, "but each pair makes me more intrigued about what's hiding underneath."

"Y-you've seen my feet," she stammered when he reached for her ankle. He slipped off the shoe, cradling her heel and pressing his thumb into the arch of her foot.

A moan escaped Alice's lips before she could stop it. As much as she favored fancy heels, they did often leave her feet sore. "That feels nice," she whispered, closing her eyes to enjoy the sensation. His hands felt like heaven as they massaged, the touch alternately soft then firm.

He finished with one foot, then took off the other shoe. Alice tried not to think of his touch as foreplay, imagining his hands on other parts of her body.

But before her daydreams had time to overtake her, Flynn let out a sharp cry.

She jerked away from Charles.

"He's hungry," she said, as she scooped up the baby, embarrassed at how husky her voice sounded.

"I'll get the bottle," Charles offered, without missing a beat.

She stood with Flynn in her arms, not bothering to put on her shoes. Charles shook up the formula, uncapped the bottle and handed it to Alice. She was careful to take it without touching him, not sure she could handle the contact with how sensitized she felt at the moment.

The baby guzzled happily, and Charles cleaned up the remnants of their meal.

"I can do that when he's finished."

"It's not a problem," Charles told her with a smile. "Think of it as your very own royal treatment." His grin was so cheeky she couldn't help but return it.

As Flynn finished the bottle, the band appeared on the stage. They were a bluegrass quartet. The lead singer played the banjo and was accompanied by a fiddle player, upright bassist and drummer. The crowd applauded, several couples near the front surging to their feet to dance to the spirited music.

"They're good," Charles said, putting the lid back on the picnic basket.

"Most music in Austin is good." Alice lifted Flynn to her shoulder and patted his back. "We're famous for it."

"This is Texas to me," Charles said softly, and reached out a hand to her.

Shifting Flynn to a more secure position in one arm, she lightly placed her fingers in Charles's. He spun her slowly, then gathered her close. The three of them danced together, swaying to the music as the band launched into a ballad, the fiddle player taking the lead with a resonating melody that tugged at her heartstrings.

Pale streaks of pink and orange colored the sky above

them, and Alice could just see the faint outline of the moon beginning to rise behind the stage.

"You're barely breathing," Charles whispered against her ear.

She pulled back. "I seem to have forgotten how," she said, and sucked in an almost painful gulp. "It's the music." She laughed and moved off the blanket, clutching Flynn to her chest. "The fiddle gets me every time."

Charles lifted a brow as if he knew too well that she was lying through her teeth. "Of course. The fiddle." He didn't move closer but tapped his toe in time to the music. "I like it here, Alice."

She brushed a light kiss across the top of Flynn's head. "I like it with you here, Charles." She turned away as soon as the words were out of her mouth, embarrassed at how much they revealed. This was temporary, she reminded herself as she swayed to the music with Flynn. Charles had made no promises, and she didn't expect him to. Her only connection to him was through her son, even if it felt like more every time they were together. She kept her attention focused on the band until her emotions were under control.

"Do you want to hold him?" she asked, turning to Charles after the next song finished.

He gave her a searching look, as if he wanted to say something, but in the end only nodded. "Certainly." He took the baby carefully, balancing an alert Flynn on his forearm.

"You look like you're holding a football," she told him as she slipped back into her shoes.

He made a face. "It's a rugby hold. A football is something you kick with your feet."

Alice made a show of glancing around. "You'd better

not let anyone in Texas hear you say that. We take our American football seriously around these parts." She purposely put an extra bit of twang in her tone. "They'll run you out of the state quicker than you can say 'God save the queen.'"

"Don't listen to her, young man," Charles cooed at the baby. "Stick with Daddy and I'll teach you what's what with sports." He looked up at Alice and winked. "He's quite awake for it being so late."

She couldn't resist taking a step closer and reaching out to trace a finger along Flynn's soft cheek. Her wonder at her son never waned, no matter how tired or stressed she felt. But being here with Charles, it was easy to forget all those troubles. "He likes watching you," she murmured.

"Or maybe it's the fiddle," Charles said, and she could hear the teasing note in his voice.

She crossed her arms over her chest and tapped a finger against her chin in mock seriousness. "Yes, we've established that the fiddle is thrilling."

"Thrilling," he repeated.

She nodded. "In a *friendly* sort of way."

He let out a bark of laughter that made Flynn jump. The baby's face contorted as he let out a wail. "I mucked that up," Charles said.

Alice automatically reached for the baby, but Charles shook his head. "Mind if I try to quiet him?"

"Sure." She watched, emotion wrenching her heart as he rocked the baby to the beat of the music. Charles might blend in with the crowd in his American clothes, but to her he still looked like the British playboy she'd read about for years in the tabloids. He was someone who had every advantage that money could buy, but here he was, trying to fit into her world—her son's world—even as he was so clearly out of his depth.

How could she resist falling in love with him?

At the thought, Alice stumbled back a step. This was the worst of all possible outcomes for her time with Charles and a secret she would take to her grave. But it wasn't the Charles Effect or his charm and natural affinity with women that had done her in. It was these small moments of sweetness and authentic emotion when he wasn't relying on his reputation. She saw Charles for who he was, flaws and all, and that was the man she loved.

But he was still the man she would never have.

Despite how she'd tried to guard it, her heart splintered into tiny pieces at the thought.

Chapter Eleven

"Have you lost your handsome British mind?"

Charles paused midbite to glance at the black-and-white photos thrown onto the table before him. He'd stopped in the hotel restaurant to grab a quick breakfast before heading over to the Texas Tourism Board office.

It was a bit disturbing how much he wanted to see Alice, especially after having spent most of the previous evening with her. Despite her protests that she was fine, he'd insisted on walking her and Flynn home from the concert, then had taken a cab back to his empty hotel room.

She hadn't invited him in, and he didn't blame her. He'd been the one to throw down the "friend" gauntlet, but no matter how he tried to convince himself it was for the best, he hated it. It was easier to think that was why he craved being close to her—she was an itch that he hadn't been able to properly scratch.

But what if that wasn't the whole story?

Normally Charles tired of women quickly, and not just in the bedroom. Alice was different. He was crazily attracted to her, but even without acting on that desire, Charles enjoyed being with her. She talked to him like he was a real person. She teased him and flirted without even realizing what she was doing. Flynn was a huge motivator, as well, and Charles wanted more time with both of them. For a man who'd done his best to avoid commitment for most of his life, all he hoped for now was that Alice would give him a chance to prove he could change.

Because he could, except...

"What the hell is the meaning of this? Did you have me followed?" His voice was stiff and dripped with contempt as his gaze shot up from the pictures. As much as he loved the image of the three of them as a happy family, this was a violation of the worst sort. But it wasn't a slimy paparazzo or tabloid reporter who stood in front of him.

The woman who stared down at him regally from the other side of the table was the epitome of class and style. She was clearly older, although nary a wrinkle marred her porcelain complexion. It was as if she had refused to allow something so trivial as the passage of time to mark her. There was an air of power around her that few would defy, but Charles had never been one to cower when faced with an outright challenge.

"Kate Fortune," he said with a practiced smile, placing his fork on the white tablecloth. "I was wondering when you would grace me with your presence."

"You can save that suave charm for one of your high-society groupies, Charles." She tapped a manicured finger on the table. "If my people can so easily deduce your identity, despite your American disguise, it won't be long until your secret is out."

Charles pressed his lips together. "I want privacy while I'm in Texas," he said through clenched teeth. "There's no secret to discover beyond that."

She arched one fine brow. "Are you going to invite me to join you?"

"Of course," he said, standing and pulling out the chair next to him. "Please have a seat, Ms. Fortune. Would you like a menu? The waffles are quite good."

"No waffles," she answered with a small chuckle, her expression softening a bit. Lucie had told him Kate had remained in Austin longer than she'd planned because she'd fallen ill and the doctor suggested her recovery would be easier in Austin than at home in Minneapolis during the brutal Minnesota winter. As Charles studied her, he noticed her silk suit seemed to be too big for her tiny frame.

"I'm still strong enough to manage both my company and my own affairs," she told him, as if reading his mind.

"And your family?" he asked.

"Cheeky boy," she muttered.

"That's what my mother always told me."

Kate draped the cloth napkin across her lap and signaled the waiter for a cup of coffee. "I like you more than I expected."

Charles tilted his head, acknowledging the compliment. "Then I'll strive to continue to exceed your expectations."

"From what I understand, that would be a rare feat for you."

"Were you this charming with the rest of the Fortune offspring?"

She smiled at the question. "Certainly not. I tailor my conversation to each individual."

"You spoke with Lucie recently," he observed.

"Your sister is a lovely girl. She takes after your mother."

"Indeed she does."

"I wonder if you are very much like your father."

Charles felt himself stiffen and had trouble keeping his gaze neutral. "What do you know of Sir Simon?"

"I know he was a good man and an even better father. I've done my research on all branches of the Fortunes, and you British lot have spent so much time in the spotlight that it's easy to gather facts on you."

"The tabloids often don't tell the whole story, if any portion of it."

One side of her mouth curved as she sized him up. "Does that mean you're not a charming rake with a raging Peter Pan complex who skated by on your looks and family name for the better part of your life?"

"I… It doesn't… There hasn't been… I don't have a Peter Pan complex." Charles broke off as he struggled to keep his breathing normal. He darted looks to the tables on either side of them, but it appeared no one had overheard Kate's scathing assessment of his worth. He wasn't sure whether to be outraged, embarrassed or some combination of the two, since this virtual stranger had concisely summed up his existence in a well-placed verbal attack.

Kate paused as a cup of steaming coffee was set in front of her. She added a scant dollop of cream and stirred, then carefully removed the spoon, setting it neatly on the saucer. Charles got the impression that Kate Fortune was methodical about every move she made, and it was no accident that she'd sought him out after discovering his connection to Alice and Flynn. The thought made an unfamiliar wave of protectiveness roll through him, crashing through his shored-up defenses like a river breaching a dam.

Before he could voice his concerns, Kate held up her hand. "I'm not going after you, Charles." She flipped the pictures over so the images were hidden from view. "My goal is to secure the future of Fortune Cosmetics. I need someone who can work with me to learn the business and dedicate him- or herself to the company the way I have."

Charles pushed his plate to the side, his normally hearty morning appetite ruined. "That isn't me."

"Are you asking or telling?" Kate retorted.

"A bit of both, I suppose. I'm not interested in running your cosmetics company, and you don't think I have it in me to dedicate myself to the business."

She studied him over the rim of her coffee mug. She clearly wore lipstick, skillfully applied like the rest of her makeup, but not a trace had bled onto the white porcelain of the china cup. Everything about Kate Fortune was perfect. "As I said, I've done my research. You are actually quite an asset to the British tourism industry. Despite outward appearances, I think you take your role as an unofficial ambassador very seriously."

Charles released a breath, relieved that the formidable cosmetics maven hadn't skewered him again.

"But," she continued, setting the cup back on the table, "I wonder if you truly understand the value of family and the commitment it takes to maintain ties with the people nearest to you."

"I'm committed to my son," he said, gripping the edge of the table so hard his knuckles turned white. "Since I found out about Flynn, I've been more dedicated to him than I have with anything or anyone before in my life. Arrangements have been made for his future, ensuring that he will always be taken care of no matter what. I put my own plans on hold to stay in Austin and spend time with him. I plan to be a part of his life going forward." Charles forced himself to relax his fingers, running a hand through his hair. "I may never measure up to Sir Simon, but I'm bloody well going to be the best father I can to that boy. No matter what you or anyone else thinks about me."

She reached out and patted his hand, as if placating a small child. "Don't get all riled up on my account. I'm not talking about your son. It's easy to love a baby."

Charles nodded. It had certainly been simple to become enamored of his son. And as for Alice—

"But family connections through the generations are just as important," Kate continued, before he could fully wrap his mind around his feelings for Alice. "They aren't always neat or easy, but it's essential to maintain those ties."

He focused on her words and on what Lucie told him had been developing within the Fortune family. "Do you include the Robinsons in those family ties?"

Kate's eyes widened a fraction. "That's a complicated situation."

"Indeed, but in the name of family, they are just as important as any of the rest of us."

She frowned, as if considering that. "My sources tell me that Ben Robinson has tracked down Jerome Fortune's mother."

"I've heard that, as well." Charles didn't volunteer any of the other information Lucie had shared.

"Jacqueline Fortune, Jerome's mother, insisted that her son is dead." Kate's expression was carefully neutral.

"Do you believe that?"

Kate shook her head. "I don't. Do you?" She leaned forward, her eyes narrowed, waiting for his answer.

"No," Charles said after a moment. "But as you say, it's complicated. I realize how lucky I am to have had the father I did. Not all children have that, and from what I understand Gerald Robinson was not the easiest man to have as a parent." Charles didn't know much about the scion of Robinson Tech and had met only a couple of the Robinson children at a charity function the previous year. Lucie had become friends with Vivian Blair, who was now engaged to Wes Robinson, who was in charge of research and development at the powerful computer company. His sister had wanted to pepper him with details about the relationships within that family, but Charles had too much going on in his own life to worry about a different branch of the Fortunes.

"He won't admit that he's really Jerome," Kate said, her mouth thinned to a worried line.

"But his children are convinced he is," Charles said softly. "They have reason to make a claim on the Fortune name beyond wanting to know the truth."

"The Fortune name holds a lot of weight in many areas."

"So does the Robinson name," Charles countered. "They don't need the money and it can't be easy to go up against a man as complicated as Gerald."

"Jerome," Kate corrected.

Charles nodded. "We're in agreement on his true identity."

"Perhaps we agree on more than just that," Kate murmured.

"Like that I'd be a terrible choice to take over your business."

She laughed, a throaty chuckle, and her eyes sparkled in enjoyment. "You really are a scamp, Charles Fortune."

"A lovable one, I hope."

She arched one sculpted eyebrow. "I've heard that, as well." Kate reached for her purse and pulled out a small velvet pouch. "I have something for you. It's been in the Fortune family for many years."

Charles automatically shook his head. "I can't take—"

"You can take what I offer to you," Kate said, her tone as regal as any aristocrat Charles had met. "And be grateful."

"Yes, ma'am," he said, quietly chastised.

She slid the velvet case toward him. "Open it."

He gently pulled out a glittering emerald engagement ring with brilliant smaller diamonds surrounding the center stone. It was clearly vintage, in an understated art deco style, and he'd guess it was worth a small fortune, to use the word in the literal sense. There was a bit of filigree outlining the top edge and he could see the letter *F* in the design. "It's beautiful," he told her with a half smile, "but not quite my size."

"It's not for you," she said with an eye roll. "But you'll need it."

An image of Alice popped into Charles's mind and his heart lurched in response. But just as quickly, a wave of fear and dread rose in his throat, almost choking him. A ring was a level of commitment he'd never imagined himself making, mainly because he knew he would disappoint the woman wearing it. If that woman was Alice and he messed up enough that she tried to deny him access to Flynn... Well, that would never work.

"I don't think so," he said, adjusting the collar of his Turnbull & Asser hand-stitched shirt. He snapped shut the pouch and pushed it in Kate's direction.

"A word of advice," she said, pushing it right back to him.

"Just one?" he quipped.

Kate smiled. "Your hair is about to catch on fire from how hard you're thinking. Keep the ring, Charles, even if you never use it. But don't think too much about it. Some things are better when they're spontaneous. Rely on your instinct."

He shook his head. "My instincts are horrible. Ask anyone who knows me."

"Alice Meyers is not your usual type," Kate said, slowly rising from the table. "Have your instincts about her been wrong?"

He stood, as well, grabbing the small ring pouch. As his fingers closed around it, the strangest thing happened. Instead of thrusting it toward Kate as he'd planned, he shoved it into his pocket.

That earned him a wide smile from the commanding cosmetics mogul.

"Just because I don't look my age," she told him, "doesn't mean I'm not wise beyond my years." She offered her hand to him.

"Ms. Fortune, it was a true pleasure," Charles said with his most courtly bow. Instead of shaking her hand, he bent over it and brushed his lips across the paper-fine skin of her knuckles.

"A scamp," she repeated, but her eyes were dancing.

"Good luck with your search for a successor," he told her as she gathered her purse.

"Thank you, Charles." She turned for the restaurant's exit, walking slowly even as the rest of the customers watched. He supposed Kate Fortune was more used to being the center of attention than he was. "Good luck with your new family," she called over her shoulder.

New family.

He mulled the words over in his mind and decided that they had a nice ring to them. Patting his pant pocket where the pouch was tucked, he sat back down to enjoy the rest of his breakfast, his appetite suddenly restored.

"I can't do this anymore." Alice dipped her french fry into a puddle of ketchup, then pointed it at Meredith. "I've gained three pounds in two weeks from stress eating."

It was Friday, the end of the workweek, and Alice had convinced her friend to go to lunch.

"It does no good to avoid him," Meredith said, forking up a bite of Cobb salad. "He keeps coming to see you, and Amanda's starting to get mad that you aren't paying enough attention to our Bonnie Lord Charlie."

"Why can't he understand that it will look suspicious if we're seen together all over town?"

"Not really," Meredith observed, "since he's working on the ad campaign with you. Julie in graphic design told me he actually has some decent ideas about the staging for some of the It's Texas spots, and that he's called in favors from every famous Texan he knows."

"That's true," Alice admitted. "He has much more insight into trends in the global tourism industry than anyone gives him credit for." She bit the tip off her fry and chewed. "But working together doesn't justify taking me to lunch every day and hovering around my cubicle at the end of the day so he can walk me to my car."

"Right." Meredith pointed her knife at Alice. "Heaven forbid someone treat you like a gentleman." She made a pretend slashing motion across her throat. "The despicable cad...off with his head."

Alice rolled her eyes. "You know what I mean, Mer. Men don't pay attention to me."

"Because other than those fancy heels you wear, everything about you screams 'Don't look, don't touch.'"

"I do not scream that," Alice protested. "Do I?"

"Why do think that condom languished in your purse for so long?"

"Because when I'm out with you, guys don't notice me."

"Charles notices you," Meredith said, her tone turning wistful. "Sometimes when we're in a meeting and someone else is talking, I'll catch him staring at you and it's..."

"What?"

"It's hot. Like the Texas plains in summer hot. Like you're a cold glass of water and he's been in the desert for months. Like—"

"Enough." Alice choked out an embarrassed laugh. She could feel her face growing warm at the thought of Charles watching her. "I get your point."

"Are you sure?" Meredith arched a brow. "Because from the circles under your eyes and the fact that you're crabby most of the time, I couldn't tell."

"I have a four-month-old baby."

"And you're sexually frustrated."

Alice clamped a hand over her mouth to stifle a gasp. "I can't believe you said that out loud," she whispered, ducking her head and glancing around to make sure no one had overheard her outspoken friend.

"It's true," Meredith said, but thankfully lowered her voice. "Charles wants you, and you're a fool not to take him to bed again."

"It's complicated," Alice said with a heavy sigh. "And he doesn't want more complications. You know limiting what's between us to friendship was his idea." She took a long drink of her sweet tea. "I need to honor that."

"You need to tempt him more."

"I need to respect his wishes." Alice shook her head. "If something happens between us and it affects his relationship with Flynn, I'd never forgive myself."

"Do you really think you'll be able to live like this for the next eighteen years?"

"I have to," Alice said, dropping her head into her hands. "It will get easier."

"In your dreams." Meredith popped a cherry tomato in her mouth. "Is he coming to the cocktail party tonight?"

"Yes," Alice mumbled. The Texas Tourism Board was hosting an event to celebrate the start of the summer vacation season. They'd rented an up-and-coming art gallery in a trendy neighborhood east of downtown. Many of Austin's prominent businesspeople and civic leaders would be attending. Charles, of course, was on the list.

"Will he be wearing a tux?"

"Probably."

"Then it sure won't get easier anytime soon." Meredith winked. "That man is lethal in a tux."

"You look lovely, sweetie," Lynn Meyers said as she took the diaper bag from Alice and carried it down the hall toward the kitchen. The cocktail party was set to start in an hour, so Alice had driven out to her parents' place to drop off Flynn for his first sleepover.

Alice followed with the baby carrier, and Flynn happily sucking his binky.

"Thanks for keeping him tonight, Mom. Are you sure this is okay?" Anxiety sat heavy in her stomach. "I'm sure I can pick him up later without waking him."

"Don't be silly. Your father and I are excited to have our grandson all to ourselves for the night." Her mom set the diaper bag on the kitchen table and tapped Alice's father on the shoulder. "Isn't that right, Henry?"

He started, then looked up from the book he'd been reading. "The baby's staying here? For how long?"

Lynn shook her head. "Just one night. I told you about it last week."

"Right," he mumbled, then glanced at Alice with a sheepish smile. "Sometimes I forget to pay attention."

"It's okay," she said, and bent forward to kiss his cheek.

"I hope you're going to put a sweater on over that getup," he said, eyeing her bright red dress. "You've got too much skin on display."

Alice settled Flynn's car seat on the table and glanced down at her fitted but relatively demure dress. It was a classic boatneck sheath with a red lace overlay. "The only skin anyone can see is my arms," she told her father.

"You should cover them," he said. "It gives men ideas."

"Ideas," her mother said with a scoff. "Don't be old-fashioned, Henry." Lynn unstrapped Flynn and lifted him out of the car seat. "Alice is beautiful."

"I know she's beautiful," Henry countered. "That's the problem."

"I promise it's not a problem, Dad." Alice reached for the diaper bag. "Men aren't that interested in me."

Her father pushed away from the table and stood. "At least one man was," he said, hitching a thumb at Flynn. "I may be an old geezer, but I'm aware of how babies are made."

Alice darted a pleading look at her mother.

"Henry, will you set up the portable crib I bought for Flynn? The box is in Alice's old bedroom upstairs."

"I'm on it," her dad answered, but first turned to his grandson, who was balanced in his wife's arms. "How do you feel about Civil War documentaries?" he asked, tickling Flynn's little toes.

The baby gurgled in response, making her father laugh. "Good point. We'll start with the Revolutionary War."

He stepped toward Alice and gave her a gruff hug. "Wherever you're going tonight, I have no doubt you'll be the most beautiful girl in the room."

"Thanks, Dad," Alice whispered, emotion making her voice catch. Her father might be the epitome of the absentminded professor, but she knew he loved her.

He shuffled toward the hall, then called over his shoulder, "Put on a sweater."

Lynn gave Alice a gentle smile. "He means well."

"I know."

Her mother shifted Flynn up to her shoulder. "He's also right. You *are* a beautiful woman. I can't help thinking there's something going on in your life that you aren't sharing with me."

Alice automatically shook her head. "It isn't worth mentioning."

"Has anything changed in the situation with your young man?"

"I don't have a young man, Mom."

"But there is one you want."

Alice wanted a particular one with every fiber of her being. "I want Flynn to be happy more than anything else." She pulled a piece of paper from the diaper bag's front pocket. "Here are instructions for tonight. He gets one more bottle before bed." She reached out and placed a hand on Flynn's back. "I hope he sleeps for you. He was up twice last night."

"We'll be fine," her mother assured her.

"I could come back here after the reception is over," Alice offered quickly. "You don't have to stay up, but that way I can deal with him when he wakes."

Lynn shook her head. "I can handle a night with him, Alice. Go home after your event and sleep. You're a wonderful mother, but even the best parents need a break."

"Thanks, Mom." Alice wrapped an arm around her mother's thin shoulder. "What would I do without you?"

"You'll never have to find out," Lynn whispered, returning the hug.

As excited as she was about the thought of a full night of sleep, Alice still had trouble leaving Flynn at her parents' place. She reviewed the contents of the diaper bag twice, checked that her father had set up the crib right, insisted on changing the baby's diaper and generally fussed as much as her mother would allow. Lynn finally pushed her out the door with a gentle nudge.

Alice knew Flynn was safe with her parents, and as she drove back toward downtown Austin, some of her anxiety disappeared. She even switched on her favorite radio station, cranking the volume and singing along with a catchy pop tune. A night off might be just what she needed to recharge and bring some much-needed emotional order back into her life.

By the time she arrived at the event venue, she was even mentally prepared to see Charles. Although she'd avoided him for most of the workday, she had sent a text that they should probably keep their distance at the party, so as not to attract attention or suspicion about their relationship. Every day Alice saw more of Charles in Flynn, from the boy's laughing blue eyes to the set of his chin when he was upset. If she and Charles were seen together too often, it was only a matter of time before the truth of the connection they shared would come out. She understood it would happen eventually, but Alice wanted to remain in her safe bubble with just the three of them as long as she could.

Charles hadn't responded to her text, and he wasn't at the party when she arrived. Maybe he'd grown tired of her vacillating between wanting to be with him and needing space. She certainly had. At least she'd gotten sick of the needing space part, even though she continued to tell herself it was better for all of them in the long run. Charles wasn't known for his long attention span, and she still expected him to move on to his next conquest at any time.

She'd dropped her car back at her apartment and then taken a cab to the event, so she accepted a glass of champagne from one of the passing waiters and then hung at Meredith's side as they made their way through the party. The fizzy liquid made her feel like she was drinking bubbles, and helped her relax. She even noticed a few of the men throw glances in her direction. Perhaps Meredith was right and the reason Alice didn't date, even before Flynn, was because she was too guarded when it came to men.

She looked in the mirror and still saw the shy, gangly book nerd with thick glasses and a mouth full of braces. But motherhood had changed more than her sleep patterns. It gave Alice a confidence she didn't have before. The knowledge that she was making it work, despite the difficulties of being a single mom, helped her see herself in a different light.

It was time she let other people see more of that light. She left her friend and approached the bar, squeezing in next to an attractive man who had earlier smiled at her across the room. He turned when her arm brushed the sleeve of his coat, his eyes crinkling at the corners. They were nice eyes, a warm coffee color, but nothing like the vivid blue of Charles's gaze.

"Can I buy you a drink?" the man asked, one corner of his mouth tugging up.

"The drinks are free tonight," she observed, then shut her eyes for a moment. That was his opening line, she realized, and she'd already messed it up. But the man only grinned at her.

"Then can I order you a drink tonight and buy you dinner tomorrow?" He held out a hand. "I'm Troy, and those are the most fantastic shoes I've ever seen."

She glanced at the red, strappy heels Charles had bought her and felt a pang of longing that had nothing to do with the guy standing in front of her. "Thanks," she answered. "My...they're new. I'm Alice." She placed her hand in his, expecting to feel at least a semblance of the sparks that always lit across her skin when she touched Charles.

Nothing. She ignored the disappointment that spiked through her.

"It's nice to meet you, Alice. What are you drinking?"

Alice felt a hand clamp down on her arm. "Nothing that you're ordering for her." A clipped British accent spoke from behind her.

She whirled to find Charles glowering at the man next to her.

"Charles Fortune Chesterfield," Troy said, his dark eyes widening a fraction. "Your reputation precedes you."

Charles's expression grew stonier. "As does yours, Warner." He tugged on Alice's arm. "If you'll excuse us."

"Stop," Alice sputtered, as Charles pulled her away. But before she took two steps, Troy grabbed her by the other wrist.

"Maybe she doesn't want to be excused," he said, his drawl growing more pronounced. Alice knew what that meant for a Texan. The thicker the accent, the quicker trouble was brewing.

Charles had called him "Warner," which meant that she'd been asked to dinner by Troy Warner, heir apparent to one of the largest privately held oil companies in the state. The firm was headquartered in Houston, but the Warner family were longtime supporters of the state's booming tourism business. They owned a sprawling guest ranch in the Texas Hill Country and were stake-holders in several of the state's professional sports teams.

She glanced around to see a number of people near the bar staring at them, and realized she was literally being pulled in two directions by these very different—

but very alpha—men. Stepping out of her shell was one thing, but being made a public spectacle was quite another.

"Enough," she whispered, shaking free from both of their grasps. "This is *not* a competition."

Troy leveled a look at Charles. "Are you sure about that, sweetheart?"

"Positive," she muttered as she caught Amanda's eye from the other side of the bar. Her boss's brows rose so severely they almost hit her hairline. Alice needed to defuse this situation as quickly and quietly as she could. "I'm going to walk away from both of you to powder my nose. I suggest you shake hands or do some backslapping or whatever men do when they're finished with a ridiculous display of egos."

Plastering a smile on her face, she turned first to Troy and leaned in for a polite but distant hug. She was pretty sure Charles growled in response, but she ignored the sound. "Thank you for the dinner invitation," she said softly, "but I have to decline."

"It's a pity, sugar," he said as she moved away. "My loss, I'm afraid."

Next she wrapped her fingers around Charles's muscled arm. To a casual observer it would look like a friendly squeeze, but Alice did her best to surreptitiously dig her nails into his custom-fitted tux jacket. She looked into his clear blue eyes, the sweet smile never leaving her face, and whispered, "I hope you understand why I'm going to kill you."

His opened his mouth to speak but she shook her head. "Going to powder my nose," she repeated, loud enough for the people around them to hear.

Then, with her face burning and her knees knocking, thanks to the curious stares she received, Alice hurried across the room as fast as her wobbly legs would carry her.

She bypassed the restrooms and pushed through the heavy steel fire door that exited out on the alley behind the building. The evening air was still warm, but not nearly as stifling as the atmosphere of the party.

What the hell had Charles been thinking? As far as anyone at the event knew, they were coworkers. A public scene would raise questions Alice didn't want to answer.

There was no way to avoid returning to the party, however, and she'd just about caught her breath when the steel door whooshed open. She straightened as Charles appeared in the alley, his gaze wild as it landed on her.

He stalked toward her and she started to speak, but before she could get a word out, his mouth clamped over hers. All thought dissolved under the pressure of that wholly demanding and utterly intoxicating kiss.

Chapter Twelve

Charles pulled Alice tight against him, wanting to feel every part of her. Needing to claim her. Desire, anger and frustration swirled within him, an electrifying mix only heightened by the feel of actually having Alice in his arms. His hands roamed up and down her back and hips, wanting to feel her curves, wanting to rip away the gorgeous dress and get to the beautiful body underneath.

He was tired of ignoring the passion he felt for her. Her text today suggesting in a few curt words that they feign indifference to each other at the party had settled under his skin like an itch he couldn't quite reach. Charles wasn't used to limits or boundaries and he wanted to rip through hers like the windstorms he'd read about that battered the Texas coast, leaving nothing standing in their wake.

But he respected her, cared for her. His emotions were

so mixed up he could hardly define them. All he knew was that he'd walked into the party with every intention of giving her the space she seemed to need.

Then he'd seen her at the bar with Troy Warner. Charles didn't know the oil scion well, but had seen him around town enough to know that Troy surrounded himself with beautiful women, and lots of them. Much as Charles had.

At least until Alice.

She belonged to him, and not just because they had a child together. Charles had spent a long time avoiding commitment, and he hadn't offered anything to Alice to give her reason to believe he'd changed.

But he had. Because of her. For her.

Everything else had faded away at that moment. He'd ignored the greetings of people he knew and the curious stares from those he didn't. His only goal was getting to Alice.

Now he had her, and while he wasn't planning to let her go anytime soon, he realized mauling her in a deserted alley wasn't the best plan of action for winning her heart.

He gentled the kiss, eased his hold on her, but even as he pulled back, she wrapped her long arms around his neck, her fingers tangling in the hair brushing his collar.

Her response enflamed his need all over again and it was several minutes before he thought about breaking the kiss.

In the end, Alice pulled away, her wide hazel eyes staring up at him with a need that quickly transformed to anger.

Charles didn't need his brother Oliver's gift with finances to know that didn't add up to anything good.

"I'm so mad at you," she said, smoothing her fingertips over her lips as if she could wipe away his kiss.

"I'm sorry," he offered automatically. In his experienced, a well-timed apology worked wonders with an angry woman.

Alice, however, didn't appear mollified. If anything, her expression darkened. She placed her hands on her hips and glared at him. "For what?"

He was momentarily distracted by the way that red dress hugged her curves. "Excuse me?"

"Why are you apologizing?"

He ran a hand through his hair and tried to think of an answer that would make her happy. "For what I did to set off your temper."

She rolled her eyes. "Which was?"

"Being an ass."

"That's a given." Her laugh was tight. "Can you be more specific? Or does it normally work to simply throw about placating words in an effort to get out of the doghouse?"

"Yes, actually," Charles admitted, running a finger under the collar of his starched tuxedo shirt. "I'm a bit of an expert at dodging trouble."

She continued to stare at him, the toe of one sexy-as-hell red heel tapping on the cracked pavement.

"Those shoes are amazing."

"Don't change the subject, Charles."

"Right." He took a breath, blew it out slowly and flashed her his most charming smile.

No response except a slight narrowing of her eyes.

"I'm sorry," he said again, "for making a scene when you'd asked me to act casual at the tourism event. But you should understand—"

She held up a hand. "No. No excuses. I'm finally getting a chance to prove myself at work, and I won't let you jeopardize it. It may not matter to you, Charles, but my career is important to me."

"Slow down, Alice," he said, stepping toward her. "It matters to me. You matter to me. I don't want to muck up anything, but it killed me to see Troy Warner flirting with you. I'd wager no man at that party could take his eyes off you tonight and I've never been good at sharing. You can ask my mum about that."

"I doubt every man was riveted by me," Alice said with a shake of her head. "That's silly."

"I was riveted," he said softly, taking her hand in his and lifting it to his mouth. "I still am. I can't think of anything else but you, Alice. I want to make you laugh and listen to you talk and kiss you senseless." He turned her hand over and pressed a kiss to the delicate skin on the inside of her wrist. "I want you in my bed again."

She swallowed and then licked her lips, the motion making heat weight his body. "You said we should just be friends."

"I'm a bloody idiot," he answered without hesitation.

She rewarded the comment with a half smile that made Charles feel like he'd just been awarded his own knighthood. "I don't want anyone knowing about us. It's better for Flynn that way." She paused, then added, "For all of us."

Charles wasn't sure he agreed, but there were more critical points to clarify right now. "Is that a yes?"

"I don't remember you asking a question."

"I know Flynn is with your parents tonight. Will you spend the night with me, Alice?"

He held his breath as he waited for her answer. "Yes," she whispered finally, and he reached for her again, lifting her into his arms and spinning as their mouths met. Nothing he'd ever done meant as much as hearing her say that one word. Alice wasn't the type of woman who gave herself casually. It meant something that she'd agreed to be with him. Despite his doubts and fears, he wanted to mean something to her.

Something more than friends.

"My car is with the valet," he said, when he could force himself to release her.

She laughed and shook her head. "We need to go back to the party."

"You're joking, right?"

"If we both disappear at the same time, everyone will know we're together."

"We *are* together."

"One hour." She leaned forward and whispered against his mouth, "Please."

"Very well," he conceded. "But I'm going to need a minute to collect myself."

She glanced down at the front of his pants, her eyes widening.

"It's going to be the longest hour of my life," he said with a groan.

"Sorry," she replied, the corners of her full mouth pulled down.

He kissed her again, hating to see a frown on those beautiful lips. "Never doubt that you're worth the wait, Alice." He opened the heavy door and motioned her in. "I'll meet you inside. One hour and then the real fun begins."

Charles was right, Alice thought fifty-five minutes later. This had definitely been the longest hour of her life.

She'd returned to the party and Meredith's side, shaking off her friend's questioning glance.

Amanda had tried to corner her in front of the buffet table, but Alice had managed to stay engrossed in conversation with various tourism board supporters, knowing her boss couldn't fault her for schmoozing with their clients and guests.

It was a wonder Alice managed to follow the thread of any conversation when her skin continued to prickle and butterflies danced across her middle each time Charles caught her eye. They stayed on opposite sides of the room. Physical distance was the only way to make it through the minutes they'd agreed to spend at the event.

She hadn't even minded when she'd noticed him talking to Amanda, her buxom boss giving off so many signals she might as well be wearing a neon placard that said Take Me Home. Instead Alice had felt the imprint of Charles's mouth on hers long after she'd reapplied lipstick and rejoined the party.

She might not be able to envision a future with the ruthlessly single Brit, but she knew he wanted her for tonight. There had been a moment when she'd considered denying his request to spend the night with him. Alice's heart was far more involved than she'd ever intended. The pain that was sure to come when Charles tired of her could affect not only her, but Flynn, as well.

But there was simply no way she could resist Charles, impending heartache or not. She didn't fool herself into thinking she could get him out of her system in one night, but she would take what she could get for now.

Live in the present moment and worry about the consequences later.

Of course, the last time she'd been with Charles, the consequences had changed her life.

Deep in thought, she started when a waiter tapped her shoulder.

"Ms. Meyers?" he asked.

"Yes, that's me. Is everything okay? Does Amanda need something?"

"I was asked to give this to you." He slipped a note-card into her hand and ducked away.

She unfolded the piece of paper and smiled at the words written in bold script inside.

"The longest bloody hour of my life is over. Meet me out front."

A smile curved her lips as she refolded the note and glanced around the crowded room. Meredith was laughing with a group of their coworkers, and Amanda sat at the bar next to Troy Warner, her hand on the attractive bachelor's arm.

Alice made her way out of the party and through the front door. A valet stood by a wooden stand. As soon as he saw Alice, the man pointed up the street. Charles's Mercedes sat a half block away, parked by the curb, the front passenger door open.

She took a step toward it, then looked back over her shoulder. "How did you know who I was?"

The older man grinned and tapped the brim of his valet cap. "Mr. Fortune Chesterfield told me to look for a beautiful woman in a red dress."

"Oh." Alice smoothed her hand over the red lace. "Well, thank you, then. Have a good night."

"You, too, ma'am."

Alice hurried toward the Mercedes and slipped into the rich leather seat. Charles smiled at her. "Hello, Alice."

"Hi," she said, her voice no more than a squeak.

"I would have waited for you directly out front, but I didn't want anyone to see us together."

"Good idea," she said as she fastened the seat belt across her lap. After a moment, she glanced at him. "Why aren't we leaving?"

He winked. "You might want to shut your door first."

She giggled. "Of course." She reached for the door and closed it. The interior of the car felt suddenly intimate.

Charles reached for her hand. "You don't have to be nervous, Alice. Nothing is going to happen tonight that you don't want."

"That's why I'm nervous," she answered. "Because I want everything."

His grin widened. "In that case," he said, revving the luxury car's powerful engine, "we'd better get going."

It took only a few minutes to drive to the posh hotel where Charles had a room, the same hotel he'd stayed at during their last encounter. One of the Four Seasons' valets opened Alice's door after they pulled to a stop under the portico that shaded the front entrance. Charles was around the car in a few seconds. He took her elbow and began to steer her inside.

Alice felt stiff and unsure, suddenly nervous about not only the wisdom of spending the night with Charles, but whether she could live up to his expectations. One night with a virtual stranger, even one as handsome as Charles, had been nothing compared with the pressure of being with someone she truly cared about. A man she loved.

As if sensing her mood, Charles spun her toward him before they'd taken two steps. His kiss was soft and coaxing, filling her senses until she felt almost boneless with desire. She melted into him, holding on to his broad shoulders for support. After a minute he lifted his head, those blue eyes gone stormy gray. "Better?" he asked, with one last kiss to the corner of her mouth.

She nodded. "I want this to be good, Charles, and—"

"It will be perfect, Alice, because it's you and me." He laced their fingers together and led her into the hotel lobby. "Will you trust me? Trust us?"

She gave another jerky nod, unable to speak around the emotion in her chest. Instead, she took in the interior of the hotel. The last time she'd been here with him it had been late at night, and she'd had enough to drink that she'd barely noticed the beautiful decor.

The walls were an antique beige with expensively patterned wallpaper, dark mahogany trim giving the impression of a classic country club. Everything about the space screamed money and understated style. As in many exclusive hotels, the staff were professional and discreet, purposely not looking as Charles led her through the lobby toward the bank of elevators on one side. When she'd come here with him a year ago, Alice had felt like Julia Roberts in *Pretty Woman*, wholly out of her element in the posh surroundings.

But tonight, as she held tight to his warm, strong hand, Alice realized the feeling bubbling to the surface inside her was belonging. Whatever happened tomorrow, tonight she belonged with Charles—in his arms and in his bed.

They stepped into a waiting elevator and he punched the button for the top floor. He turned to her as the door slid closed, his gaze questioning as if he still didn't trust her decision to come with him tonight.

Before he could speak, she pressed her mouth to his,

putting all the things she wasn't ready to say into the kiss. He responded in an instant, turning her so her back was against the cool wall of the elevator. His mouth was frenzied, trailing kisses from her lips to the line of her jaw and lower to her throat. His fingers moved aside the sleeve of her dress and his palm splayed across the top of her breast.

She sucked in a breath, arching into him, just as the elevator chimed.

"Just a few more steps," he whispered, straightening her dress.

She was dizzy with need as she followed him down the hall. He fumbled in his pocket for the room key, and it bolstered Alice's confidence to see that his fingers trembled as he held it up to the lock.

He threw her a boyish smile. "You make me lose my mind."

"Good," she told him, and leaned closer.

Then the door was open and he hauled her into the room, claiming her mouth once more.

She wanted to touch him, to feel his skin under her hands. She pushed at his tux jacket as he tugged on her zipper. The result was a jumble of limbs that had them both laughing.

Charles moved back, his breathing ragged but a teasing light in his eye. "There's no hurry."

Alice shook her head, placed a hand to her pounding heart. "I'm kind of in a hurry."

"We have all night." He reached out a finger, pushed a lock of hair off her shoulder, the light touch magnified on her heated skin. "I don't want to rush, Alice. I'm going to make this perfect for you." He put his hands on her shoulders and turned her, reaching for the zipper of her red dress. She hitched in a breath as the cool air of the room whispered across her back, followed by his knuckles brushing along her spine.

Her nerves made her want to rush this before she lost her confidence. She didn't want to think about any of the other women he'd been with and how she wouldn't measure up to them.

"Only you and me," Charles whispered into the nape of her neck as he pushed the dress down her arms. It pooled at her feet, leaving her in only her bra, underpants and those red heels he'd bought for her.

She swallowed back her nerves and turned to face him. "Now you."

"I'm too busy enjoying the view," he said, his eyes roving all over her body.

"Charles, please," she said, feeling color rise to her cheeks.

His eyes darkened in response. "Your skin is so pale you blush all over. I can't wait another minute to touch you." He took a step toward her but she shook her head.

"Too many clothes," she said, pointing at him.

Immediately he tore off his jacket, then tugged at his tie and unbuttoned his shirt.

"You move fast when you're motivated," she told him as he shrugged out of his shoes, socks and pants.

"Hell, yes," he agreed, and a moment later, he was down to his boxers. She started to slip out of the heels, but he grabbed her around the waist, hauling her against his lean chest. "Not yet. I'm still enjoying them too much."

He kissed her, his tongue tangling with hers as he moved them toward the bed. He threw back the covers, then lowered her onto the cool sheets. He sat back and took one of her feet in his hands, slowly removing the red heel as he caressed her arch, then repeated the action with the other heel. He pressed his hands to the bed on either side of her hips, staring into her eyes as if searching for something. "Are you sure, Alice?" he asked, his voice unsteady. "Is this what you want?"

She almost answered "forever" because that was the truth, but she could never admit that to Charles. Instead she whispered a simple "yes," which must have been enough, because he kissed her again, his hands moving everywhere on her body. Her bra and panties were gone a minute later, followed by his boxers. He pulled a foil packet from the nightstand drawer and ripped it open with his teeth.

"Good idea for you to provide the protection this time," Alice said with a jittery laugh, suddenly feeling anxious all over again.

Charles brought his face inches from hers. "Everything happens for a reason, darling, and your sentimental condom was no exception." He kissed her long and hard, then thrust into her, making her gasp his name.

He gave an answering moan, then Alice lost all ability to think. Her body took over, moving with Charles as if they'd been together for years. He knew exactly how to touch her, what to whisper, the way she wanted to be held. When the pressure built and finally broke over them like a sparkling wave, like every bit of sunshine and light she'd ever felt, Alice knew she was ruined for any other man.

Whether her time with Charles lasted days or weeks, or even it was over after tonight, her heart would be his forever.

Chapter Thirteen

Charles lay wrapped around Alice hours later, after making love to her for a second time. He tried to calm his heart, which was pounding not because of exertion, but from the emotions tumbling around his chest like so many rocks spilling over the side of a mountain face. That's how he felt after being with Alice again—as if he were standing on a sharp precipice, about to free-fall off the edge. Adrenaline was pumping through him, and he didn't trust himself to speak, afraid of the words that would pour out of his mouth. Words that would make him seem needy and desperate, and expose the soft underside of his heart that he kept locked away.

This was sex, he reminded himself, and he'd done the same thing too many times to count, with more women than he should admit. Being with Alice should be no different.

Except it was. And that scared the hell out of him.

He wasn't willing to let her go, but he'd have to even-tually. Kate Fortune had accused him of having a raging Peter Pan complex. As offensive as the idea was, Charles hadn't ever given much thought to settling down and being responsible. His reputation, career—his whole life—was based on being the Fortune who refused to grow up. As much as he wanted to live up to his father, Charles hated the idea that he might fail. It had always been easier not to try, and the consequences of his ac-tions hadn't mattered.

But they would to Alice. He knew he could be a part-time father and a halfway decent one, but a woman like Alice deserved a man who could fully devote himself to her. Charles had always been afraid there was something inherently lacking in him—some ability to commit that had seemed to skip him in the family gene pool. If he was destined to disappoint Alice, wouldn't it be better if he never tried in the first place?

She snuggled closer and he dropped a soft kiss on her bare shoulder as he sifted her spun-silk hair through his fingers.

"Thank you for tonight," she said softly, and he could hear the sleepy smile in her voice.

He made what sounded even to his own ears like a Neanderthal grunt. Where had his gallant polish gone now that he needed it most?

Her whole body stiffened when the silence drew out between him. "Should I go?" she asked, clearly inter-preting his inability to form a coherent sentence as dis-interest.

Yes, he wanted to yell, *go before I mess this up or hurt you or reveal so much that you hurt me.* He was so wrapped up in his own doubts that he didn't register that she'd moved out of his arms until the bed shifted. He grabbed her before she stood, and pulled her back onto the bed, lifting himself above her.

"Stay." His tone was too gruff, he knew, and she turned her face to the side.

"It's okay, Charles. You don't have to say—"

He smoothed his hand along her cheek and tipped it until she met his gaze. "I should say so much more, but my brain appears to have been addled by the best shag of my life."

The corner of her mouth lifted slightly, but was enough to give him a glimmer of hope that he could make this right.

"The best?"

"If there was a better than the best, you would be it." He kissed the tip of her nose. "I'm sorry I made you feel anything different. Stay with me tonight, Alice. I want to wake up next to you tomorrow. I want to open my eyes and see your beautiful face."

Her smile broadened. "Okay."

"Tell me it was better than okay for you?"

She tapped one finger to her mouth. "I don't have much for comparison…"

He flipped onto his back and took her with him. "Maybe you need more to compare it to?"

"Maybe I do," she agreed, and kissed him. After that, all his doubts melted away in the heat and light of Alice.

Although he'd asked her to stay the night before, Charles expected to be ready to say goodbye to Alice once they woke up. He liked a solitary morning, usually needing to recover from his active nighttime social life.

But once again, being with Alice was a revelation.

He was not only happy to have her body curled around him, he wanted to spend as much of the day as he could with her. He watched her sleep, her breath easing in and out. She was on her side, facing him, the sheet bunched under her arms with just the tips of her breasts showing. She'd washed off her makeup sometime in the night and in the morning light he could see a faint dusting of freckles across her nose. He wondered if Flynn would have his mother's freckles and her sweet spirit. Charles couldn't wait to see how his son developed.

He also couldn't seem to wait for Alice to wake up. Charles trailed his finger along her collarbone, then down her chest, curling his fingertip in the sheet to tug it down.

Alice's eyes flew open as her hand clamped over his.

"Good morning," he said, bending his head to press his lips to the swell of her breast.

"Hi," she said with a small yelp of pleasure. "You're up early."

"Every day, love."

"Now I see where Flynn gets his sleep habits." She yawned, then yelped as Charles nipped at her skin. "I need coffee."

"I have something to wake you up faster than caffeine." He pulled at the sheet again. "It's going to be your best morning ever."

She stretched her arms around his neck, and his muscles heated in response. "Let's see what you've got."

After a leisurely breakfast ordered from room service and a shower, Alice insisted she needed to go back to her apartment to change and then pick up Flynn from her parents.

"I'll drive you," Charles offered, pulling on the Keep

Austin Weird T-shirt that was quickly becoming his favorite.

"To my apartment?" Alice asked, slipping on the red heels from the previous night. He wanted to buy her those shoes in every color and beg her to wear them for him each night. "Thanks, that would make the walk of shame I'm about to do less embarrassing."

"No shame," he told her. He paused, then added, "I could free up my schedule and take you out to your parents' house to get Flynn if you want."

The truth was, he had nothing on his calendar for the day. He'd taken to leaving it empty in the hopes that he'd get to spend time with Alice. It was easy enough to fill when he needed to, and most of his friends and family would be shocked to see him rearranging his plans for a woman. At this point, he didn't care.

But the look Alice threw him from across the room definitely wasn't encouraging.

"That's not a good idea."

"Why?"

"My mom and dad don't know anything about…" She squeezed her fists at her sides. "About Flynn's father."

"You mean me?"

"We agreed to keep this private, Charles."

"For how long?" he asked, grabbing his wallet and keys from the dresser and shoving them in his pocket. "My brothers and sisters know I have a son now. They aren't going to tell anyone outside the family. I assume your parents aren't going to phone it in to the tabloids."

"Of course not."

"Then why can't I meet them?"

She took a step toward him. "Because they would have expectations for you and me. I love my parents, but they're traditional. It was difficult for them to come to terms with me becoming a single mother. I can't just waltz in there and introduce them to some international playboy who also happens to be my...my baby daddy."

"That's an interesting term," he said through clenched teeth.

"I'm sorry, but it's the truth."

She looked as miserable as Charles felt, and he wanted to wrap her in his arms and tell her he'd make everything right for both of them. The problem was, he didn't know how.

"Give us more time to figure things out, Charles. Unless you have the answer for how all of this is going to work."

"I'm here now," he offered, even though it sounded lame to his ears. But he couldn't give her anything more. He wasn't ready, wasn't sure he'd ever be.

Alice gave him a tight smile. "I appreciate that, but I'm not prepared for you to meet my parents. Not yet."

"Whatever you want," he said, and forced his own smile. "Let's be on our way, then."

They rode in silence to her apartment, and Charles hated every second of it. He wanted to reach across the interior of the car and take her hand. He wanted to do something to renew the feeling between them, the one that made him itchy and uncomfortable and happier than he could ever remember.

But he didn't say anything. He didn't do anything. He pulled to the curb in front of her building minutes later. "Here you go, love."

She put her hand on the door handle. After a moment she turned to him. "After his afternoon nap, I'm going to give Flynn cereal for the first time. I know it's not the most exciting way to spend a Saturday." Her smile was hesitant but did wonders for his mood. "But I'd love for you to come over and help."

"I wouldn't miss it," he said, and her smile widened.

Alice finished changing Flynn's diaper just as the doorbell rang. She hurried to put a new outfit on the baby, then carried him out to open the front door.

Charles stood on the other side, holding a cardboard box that hit him midchest. On the side was a photo of a baby in a high chair.

"You didn't have to do that," Alice said, taking a step back to make room for Charles to enter.

"You said you hadn't bought a high chair yet." He lifted it easily, his arm muscles bunching under the casual T-shirt he wore. No matter how much he dressed like an American, Charles always looked like the perfect, dashing Brit to her.

"I haven't needed one yet," she told him. "And I'm a little short on space in here."

He beamed. "That's why this one is perfect." He flipped the box around and pointed to the picture on the other side. "The saleswoman recommended it for small spaces. It folds up to only eight inches wide so you tuck it into a corner when he's finished eating." Charles leaned forward and jiggled Flynn's foot. "Hullo, little man. Are you ready for some tasty porridge?"

Flynn looked at him and broke into a smile and happy gurgling that made Alice's insides clench. Looks like she wasn't the only one enamored with Charles. But she was determined to protect Flynn's innocent little heart, even if hers was already preparing for the inevitable ache.

"Thank you. That's very generous, Charles. You don't have to lavish us with gifts every time we see you."

"Who's lavishing?" he asked with mock solemnity. "This is only the tip of the iceberg."

She went to close the front door, but he held up a hand. "I'm not kidding, Alice. There are three more bags in the hall." He propped the high chair box against the back of the couch, then stepped around her.

Alice's eyes widened as he pulled several large shopping bags with a local toy store's logo printed on the sides into the apartment. "What more could we need?"

"According to the saleswoman, quite a bit. The developmental milestones come fast in the next few months, so I've got board books and teething rings and activity toys for every occasion."

Flynn watched Charles unload the bags with interest. Alice was still in shock. "You don't need to do this."

"But I want to." He reached for the big box again. "Let's get this thing set up so we can start our boy on some yummy…" He paused, flashing her a sheepish smile. "What is it he eats again?"

"Rice cereal."

"Sounds tasty."

Charles tipped the box flat on the floor, then lifted his arms. "I'll take him for a bit."

"Are you sure?"

"He can read the assembly directions to me."

Alice laughed but grabbed a small fleece blanket from the arm of the sofa and spread it onto the floor. "He's four months old," she said as she laid Flynn on the soft fabric.

"Then we'll have to wing it."

Flynn kicked his arms and legs as if he was excited by the prospect of helping his daddy with a project.

The flutter in Alice's heart as she watched her two boys together felt both familiar and sweet. Even if the scene before her wasn't entirely true. Charles wasn't hers, as much as it had felt like it last night. Yet he was here now, and Alice was becoming quite an expert at living in the moment and burying her deeper needs and desires.

She mixed together the dry cereal and water until it was the soupy consistency Flynn's pediatrician recommended. By the time she had turned from the counter, Charles was setting Flynn into the high chair.

"That was quick."

"Turns out they come almost assembled. There's one problem, however."

She took a step closer and smiled. Flynn's face was eye level with the high chair tray, his little head drooping to one side. "He may need to grow into it a bit."

"A bit," Charles agreed, and they shared a grin that she imagined parents all over the world could appreciate. It was the amusement of two people united in their love for a baby, which made even the littlest moments special.

She found a blanket to prop Flynn up, then adjusted the straps of the high chair until he looked comfortable.

Charles picked up the bowl of cereal from the table and stirred it a few times. "This doesn't look edible."

"It is for babies." She arched an eyebrow. "Unless you want to taste test it first?"

"That sounds like a dare, Ms. Meyers."

She pulled a spoon out of one of the kitchen drawers and pointed it at him. "Are you up for the challenge?"

With a cheeky grin, he took the spoon from her and dipped it into the cereal. "Only for you," he told her, then took a bite.

She couldn't help but smile as she watched him. How

many other people had seen this playful, casual side of Charles? Probably his mother and siblings. Maybe friends from school. But Alice wondered if he'd let down his guard with any other women before her. It wasn't something that came natural to him, so she doubted there could be many.

"Hey." He touched a fingertip to her nose, making her jump. "I'm the one supposed to be making faces here."

She shook off her musings. "How was it?"

"Not bad, but not good, either." He turned to Flynn, who was watching the exchange with wide eyes. "What do you think, wee man? Ready for a go at it?"

As if in response, Flynn slapped his palms on the plastic tray. Charles started to hand the bowl to Alice, but she shook her head. "Do you want to give him the first bite?" she asked.

"Are you sure?"

Every moment she'd had with Flynn had been on her own. She'd changed diapers, soothed him, witnessed his first smile and listened to his first baby babbling by herself. That's how she'd wanted it. She'd needed to prove to herself and to her parents and friends that she could manage things on her own. That she was more than anyone thought she was.

But that was just one more way Charles was different. He expected her to be the expert on parenting. And in many ways she was, although she was no longer alone. Even if it couldn't be as much as she wanted, she and Charles were partners and connected for life by their beautiful son.

So she was happy to let him take the lead on his "first" first.

She nodded and he turned to Flynn. "Let's make your

mommy proud, Flynn, my boy." He scooped up a small bit of cereal and held it out to the baby. Flynn opened his mouth automatically as the spoon got closer and Charles dipped it between his rosebud lips.

Immediately Flynn pulled back, scrunched up his face and shuddered.

Alice held her breath and Charles froze, waiting to see the rest of the reaction.

After a moment, the baby's features softened and he smacked his lips together, then opened his mouth for more. "Well done, lad," Charles said with a laugh, and fed him another bite.

Alice took over, and eventually Flynn turned away from the spoon, signaling he was full. She put the bowl and spoon into the sink as Charles lifted him out of the high chair. She watched Charles grab a wipe from the container on the table and dab it at Flynn's cheeks. Something about the way he held the baby made Alice melt even more than usual. It was late afternoon and she wanted nothing more than to grab Charles and pull him close, to lean into his strength.

That was dangerous. Heartache was one thing to deal with, but a complete break was too much. She would save that for when she was safely alone again.

"Do you want to do something fun?" she blurted before she passed the point of no return.

Charles rocked Flynn gently in his arms. "What did you have in mind?"

"Bats," she said.

Charles cocked a brow. "Bats?"

"They're a thing in Austin. The world's largest urban bat colony lives under the Congress Avenue Bridge downtown—over a million bats. They migrate down to

Mexico for the winter but come back each March. Every spring and summer night around sunset they take off for their evening feeding. It's pretty amazing to see."

He didn't look convinced.

She pointed to his chest. "You're wearing a Keep Austin Weird T-shirt. It's time to prove you believe it."

"Another challenge?" Charles grinned. "I like it. Lead on, my dear."

Alice was always surprised there were locals around town who hadn't ever visited the bats. Maybe her family was quirkier than most, but when she was a kid they'd packed a picnic at least once a month during the summer and come downtown for the evening display. She loved the nightly ritual and had watched it become a popular tourist attraction.

But Alice still remembered her dad's secret parking space near the bridge, and guided Charles to it. They parked, then pulled out the stroller and attached Flynn's infant carrier to the top. Joining the small crowd of people moving toward the bridge, she and Charles walked in comfortable silence. To passersby they were just another family on their way to witness one of the city's more unique attractions.

They found a spot just off the path near the edge of the bridge, near the place Alice had stood so many times with her parents. The sky was streaked with ribbons of pink and purple as the sun set behind the nearby buildings.

Above the noise of people they could hear a high-pitched chirping. "Bats?" Charles asked.

Alice nodded, then smiled as he tightened the sun cover over Flynn's car seat.

"He's safe," she said gently.

"No use taking chances," Charles answered, before wrapping an arm around her shoulder.

Just then the sound of fluttering wings filled the air, and a mass of bats flew out from below the bridge, black against the pink-and-purple sky as they streaked across it in an undulating pattern.

She heard Charles suck in a breath as he pulled her closer. "Amazing," he whispered into her hair, and Alice felt a wash of contentment roll through her.

Everything about this moment was amazing. Never, in all the times she'd been here with her parents, had she ever imagined standing in the same place with her own family. Temporary as it might be, she would remember it forever. The feeling of belonging with Charles was something she'd never be able to replace.

After the bats had flown off for the night, the three of them made their way back to her apartment. Flynn was asleep in his car seat, and she quickly changed him and put him to bed for the night. Charles was waiting by the front door when she came out, his hands stuffed in the front pockets of his jeans.

"That was one of the best evenings out I've had in a long time," he told her.

"You're lying," she said with a laugh, "but I appreciate it, anyway."

"It's the truth, Alice." He stepped forward and cupped her cheeks with his hands. "Anything we do together makes it the best." His mouth brushed lightly against hers, but when she stepped into him, he pulled away.

"I should go." He shoved his hands into his pockets again. "I'm sure you want some rest while the baby is down." He backed toward the door, a half smile curving his lips. "If I stay, I'm afraid you won't get much sleep."

She should let him leave but couldn't stand the thought of this night ending. She wanted to lose herself in him again. To continue what they'd started last night and claim as much time with him as she could.

"Sleep is overrated," she said, and reached for him.

His hand stilled on the doorknob. "You don't have to do this."

"I want to, Charles." She ran her palms up the hard planes of his chest even as his body remained like a statue beneath them. It was difficult for her to take the lead. Being assertive wasn't part of Alice's nature, but this man was worth the effort. Being a mother had changed her, and in some ways Charles had changed her, too. Although he didn't move, she knew he wanted her. Last night had been real and it gave her the confidence to thread her fingers through his hair and pull his face down to hers. "I want you."

Those three words seemed to release something in him, because the next thing she knew, Alice was in his arms and he was heading for her small bedroom. "Right now, my sole aim in life is to make you happy." He kissed her, running his tongue across the seam of her lips.

"This is a very good start."

Chapter Fourteen

The next morning, Charles sat at the small table in Alice's kitchen, Flynn in his arms. The baby had finished a bottle, let out a huge burp and was now sucking on his fist as he gazed up at Charles.

Alice set a plate with a toasted bagel and half a banana on the table. "Sorry I don't have anything more."

"This is great," Charles told her, and, surprisingly, he meant it. He lived out of hotels more weeks than not and was used to big breakfast buffets or ordering room service. But this quiet morning waking up with Alice and Flynn was the best he'd had in ages. So good, in fact, that he didn't want it to end.

"I've been thinking…" he said, as Alice sat across from him, her long fingers wrapped around a steaming mug of coffee.

"Should I be worried?" she asked with a small smile.

That was another thing he loved—the more time he spent with her, the less Alice seemed to feel shy around him. She had a playful, teasing streak that most people in her life didn't get to see. The fact that he did made Charles ridiculously happy.

"I want to bring Flynn back to London with me." Charles held the boy closer as he took a bite of bagel.

Alice stared at him a few moments, then asked, "For a visit?"

"Of sorts." Flynn fussed a bit, so Charles stood and rocked him until he quieted. "Would you like to live across the pond, Flynn, my boy? Romp about Kensington Gardens and visit the London Zoo?" Charles kept his gaze on the baby even as he spoke to Alice. "It's a brilliant plan, if I do say so myself. My flat has three bedrooms, so I can easily turn one into a nursery. It will be simple enough to have my assistant make the arrangements."

"Your assistant?"

"I haven't mentioned her?" He reached for a rattle and held it up for Flynn to grab. "Mary's been with me for years. She handles all my scheduling and basically runs my life."

"You need someone to run your life?"

Charles chuckled but kept watching Flynn. "It's a busy life, my lovely Alice."

"And you want to make Flynn a part of it?"

Something in her tone made him glance away from Flynn toward the woman now standing a few feet from him, arms crossed over her pink T-shirt, one toe tapping against the carpet. "You, too, of course," he answered quickly, wondering if that's what had made her temper spike. Because there was no denying the mulish set of her jaw.

What had happened to the Alice who had been pliant in his arms all night, or the one who had sweetly cuddled Flynn between the two of them early this morning? Hell, Charles would take almost any mood in place of her anger, especially as it appeared aimed directly at him.

"As I said, there are three bedrooms in the flat. I've dropped a few hints to Amanda about loaning you and your stellar research skills to the British Tourism Council for a few months."

"You've talked to my boss?" There was a sharp edge to Alice's tone that made Charles flinch. Even Flynn seemed to notice the change and began to whimper softly.

Charles rocked the boy more vigorously as he took a step toward Alice. "Just in passing. I thought it best to lay the groundwork—"

"For me to leave my life behind?" Her hazel eyes had gone hard as stone.

"Alice, you keep posing questions that sound more like accusations. I'm doing the best I can here. Being a father is new to me, as is thinking about someone other than myself."

"By 'someone,' you mean Flynn?" she asked, her mouth barely moving as she spoke.

"And you. I understand the two of you are a package deal. If you don't feel comfortable staying at my place, I can set you up with your own apartment in the neighborhood. It's a lovely area of London with—"

Flynn let out a sharp cry and Alice moved forward before Charles could react. She scooped the baby out of his arms and held him close. The boy immediately quieted and nuzzled against her shoulder. "It's a generous offer," she said, but her voice sounded hollow.

"I mean it." Charles knew he was losing ground, but couldn't figure out why, or how to regain his footing. "I've told you before, we're a team. I'll make sure you're comfortable and taken care of. Flynn won't want for a thing."

"A team," she murmured. "I take it your assistant is part of this team, as well?"

He shrugged. "In a manner of speaking. But I'm talking about you and Flynn. The three of us."

She gave a jerky nod. "When would you want to leave?"

"I have a meeting with the director of the British Tourism Council at the end of next week that I can't reschedule. If you need more time, I can go over first and get things ready."

"Can I have a few days to think about it?"

Charles felt himself frowning. "What's there to think about? Flynn is my son and I want him—both of you—with me. I want to take care of you." He knew he was mucking this up, that whatever he was saying was pushing her away instead of bringing her closer. He wanted to scoop her into his arms and kiss her until the distance between them disappeared.

"This is new for me, too, Charles. I don't even have a passport."

"I have connections that can expedite that process."

"You have a lot of things," she said, "but all I have is my baby and my family. I need time."

He sighed. Of course she did. This was not a rejection. Not outright, anyway. He shouldn't have assumed she'd be as excited about his plan as he was. But he had, because he thought she'd felt as much for him as he did for her. Maybe that had been just wishful thinking. He was Flynn's father, but that didn't mean Alice would want anything more than help with parenting. Yes, they'd shared a few nights of passion, but that could be a new mother needing to scratch an itch, with Charles being the most convenient outlet. The idea created a sick feeling in his chest. Charles had never had to work hard for anything in his life, and certainly not the affections of a woman.

The potential for failing made him want to turn and run, but then he glanced at Alice, who stood on the far side of the small family room, watching him as she cradled Flynn in his arms.

No.

He wasn't going to take the easy way out this time. Alice and Flynn were too important. If she needed time, he'd give it to her. More importantly, he'd find a way to convince her that he was worth taking a chance on.

"Take the time you need, Alice." He moved toward her, bent and kissed the top of her forehead. "I need to visit my family in Horseback Hollow before I return to England." He ruffled Flynn's hair. "I'll ring you in a few days, and we'll discuss our plans then."

He wasn't sure he could take another argument, so before she could offer one, he turned and left her apartment. It was time to become the man his father had believed he could be.

"He walked out on you just like that?" Meredith took a long pull on her beer and shook her head. "No fight? No declaration of love?"

Alice forced herself to laugh even as embarrassment

colored her cheeks. "He said he'd call in a few days. He needs to check in with his family." She glanced at the baby monitor that sat on the coffee table, almost hoping that Flynn would let out a cry so she could have an excuse not to have this conversation. Meredith had called shortly after Charles left, and Alice hadn't been able to hide her hurt at the way the morning had ended. Her friend had brought over carryout and beer from a local brewpub. While Alice was grateful for the company, she didn't want to revisit the humiliation of Charles's earlier offer.

Meredith sniffed. "After demanding that you leave your whole life behind and follow him to England."

"It's not much of a life," Alice said quietly. "He probably thinks he's doing me a favor. I could still work, and I'm sure I'd have more help with Flynn."

"But you'd be an ocean away from your parents."

"I want Flynn to know his father."

"Alice." Meredith scooted closer on the sofa and took Alice's hands in hers. "What do you want for yourself?"

Alice stared at her friend for a moment, finding it difficult to process the deeper meaning of the question. "I told you…"

"You are an amazing mother," Meredith said softly. "I know that no one believed you could handle raising a baby on your own. We underestimated you. All of us did. Your parents, everyone at work. Me."

"It's okay."

"No. It's not." Meredith shook her head. "Although you've proved us wrong, Flynn can't be your whole life." She held up a hand when Alice would have argued. "The best thing you can do for that baby is to be happy. What is going to make you happy, Alice?"

"Charles," she whispered, before she could stop herself.

"I knew it," Meredith shouted, and jumped up from the couch.

"Meredith, quiet. You'll wake Flynn."

"It isn't just for Flynn that you want to follow Charles, is it?" Her friend sank back down, tucked her legs under her. She'd lowered her voice, but her tone was animated.

"It's not that simple."

"Why not? You want him. He wants you."

"He wants me in the same way he wants his assistant. I make his life easier."

"Is that so bad?"

"I don't want easy." Now Alice stood, paced from one side of the room and back. "You all weren't the only ones who doubted I could handle motherhood. I never thought I could do it on my own. The past year hasn't been easy, but every difficult moment has been worth it. It's made me a better person. It's changed me. I don't want to go back to depending on someone. If I go with Charles, where does that leave me? Who will I be with him?"

Meredith frowned. "You'll be Alice. Flynn's mother."

"But what if Alice isn't enough? What if I have to watch him date other women? What if he meets someone he wants to marry, when I'm…"

"In love with him?"

Alice didn't bother to argue. "I told myself not to let it happen, but I couldn't help it."

"Of course not," Meredith agreed. "He's Bonnie Lord Charlie. Half the female population is in love with him."

"You don't understand." Alice ran a hand through her hair, thought of the way Charles had fanned the strands across the pillow early this morning. "I love him despite the way the world knows him. I love him for the parts of him that no one else sees. The pieces that he doesn't even see. He's a good man, more than most people ever imagine. I know he cares about me, but it isn't enough. If I've just discovered that I'm strong enough to stand on my own, how could I ever be satisfied with half a life?"

Meredith pressed her fingers to her temples. "Then you're not going to go with him?"

Alice shrugged. "I'm not sure I can let him go."

"Heartache either way."

"Heartache seems like a pretty good option at this point." Alice felt a tear track down her cheek. "It's full-blown heartbreak that scares me half to death." And swiping at the tears with her fingertips, she sank into her friend's comforting embrace.

Chapter Fifteen

"I've been wondering when you were going to grace me with your presence, Charles."

Charles smiled and dropped a kiss on his mother's soft cheek where she sat in the cozy study of her condo outside of Horseback Hollow. The house was small and relatively casual compared to the sprawling estate where Charles had grown up, but his mother looked as regal as if she were about to take high tea with the queen. Although Josephine May Fortune Chesterfield had spent most of her life in England, she'd adapted to life in this quaint Texas town like she was made for it.

It had been only a few years ago that Josephine had discovered she was the third triplet in a trio that included James Marshall Fortune, head of the powerful Atlanta company JMF Financial, and Jeanne Marie Fortune Jones, who had raised her brood of children in Horseback Hollow. The British Fortunes had first come to the tiny town for their cousin Sawyer's wedding to Laurel Redmond, but all of them, except Charles, had eventually returned to find love in Texas.

His mother enjoyed being near her children, grandchildren and extended family. She'd even found the beginning of a new relationship with retired pilot Orlando Mendoza. She'd cut back on her philanthropic duties overseas and spent more time working with local charities now. But even with her busy schedule, Charles knew she always had time to play the family matriarch, a role she embodied with compassion, caring and only the most refined and well-intentioned measure of heavy-handedness.

"So sorry, Mum," he said, as he dropped into the chair next to her.

"Sit up straight, Charles," she said quietly.

"Right." He corrected his posture with a wink. "The state tourism board has kept me quite busy the last couple of weeks."

Josephine raised one eyebrow. "Is that all?"

"Who told you?" He narrowed his eyes. "Was it Lucie? I made her promise..."

"The question is not which of your siblings mentioned your young lady to me," his mother said. "I'm wondering why I didn't hear the news from you." She held up a hand to stave off his explanation. "More importantly, when do I get to meet this woman and my new grandson?"

"It's complicated," he muttered.

"I wouldn't expect anything else from you."

He lowered his head into his hands and took a deep breath. Although he'd been worried about his mother discovering the truth about Alice and Flynn, now it felt like a relief. Josephine was the most loving, compassionate person Charles knew, and he would have felt that way even if she hadn't been the one to change his nappies when he was a babe. He hadn't realized until now how much he wanted her advice and perspective on the unholy mess that was his current life. "I'm sorry I haven't said anything to you about the baby."

"And the baby's mother? This woman who tracked you down to tell you after the fact that you are a father?"

"Don't judge her," Charles said immediately. "The way I left things after our time together…she had no reason to believe I'd be interested in the baby. You know how the tabloids paint my life."

"I understand. The fact that you're defending her means you've made peace with the way things happened."

He gave a small nod. "Her name is Alice Meyers. We met at a tourism conference last year and she's…different than my typical girlfriends."

Josephine pressed a manicured hand to her chest. "Thank heavens for that."

"I haven't brought her to meet everyone because she's shy and I think my lifestyle makes her nervous. She's happy with a quiet night at home and doesn't come from a big family. I know she likes me… I think she likes me…" He choked out a laugh. "I want her to like me."

"Charles, you are one of the most likable people in the world. If she can't appreciate that…"

He shook his head. "That's the thing, Mum. She doesn't seem to care about what makes me popular with everyone else. It's almost a negative that I'm famous. I don't have to try with her. She doesn't care about going out or being seen with me. It's…normal."

"Normal is underrated," Josephine said, nodding.

"Your father and I wanted to give our children a regular upbringing, but it was difficult with the British press hounding us so much of the time."

Charles stood and moved to the sofa next to his mother. "You and Dad were the best, Mum. It scares the hell out of me that I won't be even a tenth of the parent either of you were."

"You have a big heart, and you want to do the right thing by your son. That counts for a lot."

"That's what Alice tells me."

"I like her already. It's also obvious that you care about her very much." Josephine tilted her head to study him. "Perhaps that's part of your difficulty."

The thing about having an amazing mother was sometimes she was so perceptive, even when Charles didn't want her to be. "I can't remember ever feeling this way about anyone. Alice matters. But I'm afraid of handling it poorly. I haven't exactly had to work hard for most of my success."

Josephine gave a motherly *tsk*. "You sell yourself short. Have you told her how you feel?"

"I asked her to come to London with me. Along with Flynn, of course. I can turn one of the extra bedrooms into a nursery."

"What is Alice going to do in London?"

"I've arranged for the Texas Tourism Board to loan her to the British council for a bit."

His mother's eyes widened a fraction. "Did she agree to that?"

"Not exactly," Charles admitted. "But she will. She has to. I can't imagine not having her and Flynn in my life."

"But from how you've explained it, that's not what you told her."

"She knows it's what I meant."

"Are you certain?"

"Of course," Charles answered, even though he wasn't certain at all. "I want to take care of her and protect her. I'd never make that kind of an offer if I didn't care about her." He glanced at the framed photos of his siblings and their families that lined the cherry bookshelf. "What do I do now?"

Josephine gave him a gentle smile. "What do you want?"

"I want a family of my own. Alice and Flynn are it for me."

His mother shifted closer, leaned forward to pat his cheek. "Just make sure she knows that, dear." She glanced at her watch and stood. "And bring them to visit before you leave Texas, if that's indeed what you decide to do. I want to meet the woman who's captured your heart."

He shook his head. "I care about her, Mum. That's different than my heart being involved."

"If that's what you need to believe," she said. "I'm meeting Orlando for an early dinner with Jeanne Marie and Deke. Would you like to join us?"

"As much as I enjoy my aunt and uncle's company, I'll take a rain check." Charles stood, as well, and gave his mother a quick hug. "I'm going out to the ranch to visit with Amelia and little Clementine."

"You're staying in Horseback Hollow for a few days, then?"

He scrubbed a hand over his jaw, realized he'd forgotten to shave this morning. "Alice told me she needs a couple of days to think about her decision regarding London. If I'm in Austin, I won't be able to stay away from her. While I'm here I'm hoping someone can help me come up with a plan to convince her that leaving with me is best for everyone."

"What if you can't?"

"Not an option. This is the most important thing in my life, and I'm going to fight for Alice and Flynn. No matter what."

Josephine cupped his cheek in her elegant hand. "Your father would be proud, Charles."

Alice was in a meeting Tuesday morning when her phone started ringing. She normally kept it with her, set to vibrate, on the days her mother babysat Flynn, in case of an emergency. But the number that flashed on the screen wasn't one she recognized, so she pressed the button to send it directly to voice mail, and focused her attention back on Amanda, who was talking about an environmental tourism initiative at the front of the room.

A moment later the vibrating started again and Alice glanced down to see three more "unknown" numbers come through. Weird.

"Alice, are we keeping you from something important?" Amanda's clipped tone rang out in the quiet room, and Alice felt like a schoolgirl called out by a reproachful teacher.

"Sorry," she muttered, and turned her phone to Do Not Disturb mode for the rest of the meeting.

She pulled it out again as she walked toward her desk thirty minutes later. Before she had a chance to check the twelve new voice mails she'd received, she noticed everyone in the office staring at her. A prickly feeling started between her shoulder blades at the attention. What had happened to have her coworkers gaping at her?

Meredith was waiting in front of Alice's cubicle, a mix of sympathy and frustration in her eyes.

"What's going on?" Alice whispered as Meredith dragged her into the small space.

"Nothing to see here, people," her friend announced to the office as a whole. "Go back to whatever you were doing. She's still our Alice."

"Of course I'm still Alice. Why wouldn't I—" She broke off as Meredith shoved her into the desk chair. The computer monitor glowed bright with the front page of a popular online gossip site. The photo was the first thing that caught her attention. It was a picture of Charles, her and baby Flynn from the evening of the park concert. Alice was holding Flynn as Charles leaned over the two of them, his arm circling her shoulders. There was no denying the intimacy of the moment, and Alice felt her heart tug as she remembered the sweetness of that night and the passion she and Charles had shared after Flynn went to bed. Then her attention jerked to the headline above the photo, written in bold, black type.

Bonnie Lord Charlie's Love Child Living in Texas.

Oh, no.

Her gazed jerked to Meredith's. "Everyone knows."

Her friend gave a small nod. "It hit while you were in the meeting. Almost all the online tabloids have picked up the story. The office phone has been ringing off the hook and the receptionist called building security to stand watch at the front door." She shook her head. "The paparazzi are waiting for you outside."

Alice's chest constricted painfully and she bent forward, gasping for breath. "This is my worst nightmare, Mer."

"I know, sweetie. I'm sorry."

"No." Alice shot out of the chair, punched at the screen of her cell phone with trembling fingers, then grabbed her keys and purse. "Flynn is with my mom. I've got to get to my parents' house before the reporters do."

"Alice, we need to talk."

She glanced over her shoulder to see Amanda standing in the opening of her cubicle.

"I need to speak to you in my office. Now," her boss announced.

Alice gulped back the panic choking her throat. "I can't."

Amanda crossed her arms over her designer blazer. "Is it true? Is Charles your baby's father?"

"Yes," she whispered as she stepped forward.

"How did it happen?"

"I'll give you a lesson on the birds and bees later," Meredith answered for her. "Right now, Alice needs to get to Flynn."

Amanda shook her head and something besides panic welled in Alice. Determination. "I'll go through you if I have to," she said with more calm than she felt. "But I'm leaving to get to my son right now."

"Not out the front door." Amanda hitched a thumb over her shoulder. "The sidewalk is teeming with reporters. They'll never let you through."

Alice had parked in a lot around the corner from the tourism board office because it was cheaper than the covered garage attached to the building. "How am I going to get to my car?" she said with a desperate sob.

"Take mine," Amanda offered immediately, then

looked from her to Meredith. "No need to gawk at me. I'm not a total monster."

"I never thought you were," Alice told her honestly, "but thank you."

"Come on, I'll grab the keys for you." She ushered Alice through the office, and no one dared make eye contact, with Amanda leading the way. "I'm impressed," she said, as she pulled a key fob out of her purse. "I never thought you had it in you to nab a Fortune."

"That wasn't my intention," Alice said, knowing people around the world now thought of her as an ambitious gold digger. "I wanted my son to know his father. If it weren't for—"

"Enough." Amanda tossed the keys to her. "I was joking. No one who knows you would ever believe you were capable of being that opportunistic."

"Plenty of people who will think it, anyway."

"Forget them," Amanda advised. She took a tube of lipstick from her purse and reapplied it quickly. "I'm going to go out front and distract the paparazzi." She flashed Alice a calculated smile. "I've always wanted to be on camera. You hurry out to the garage before anyone catches on that you've left."

Alice nodded. "Why are you doing this?"

"I like to give you a hard time, but you're good at your job and I know you're a fantastic mother." She pointed at Alice. "There was also a spark so bright between you and Charles Fortune Chesterfield it could set fire to wet logs."

Charles. Alice knew he'd gone to Horseback Hollow to visit his family before returning to England. She'd asked for time to think about his proposal that she accompany him to London, and couldn't help but wonder if he'd changed his mind during his time away. After all, he was used to women falling at his feet, not questioning him. Had the press tracked him down in the tiny Texas town where most of his family lived? None of the Fortunes were fans of the paparazzi, and they wouldn't welcome the intrusion into their lives. How would they feel about the woman who'd caused it?

Her breath caught again, but she didn't have time to worry about Charles or the rest of the Fortunes now. She had to get to Flynn.

True to her word, Amanda distracted the reporters so Alice could escape. As she pulled out of the garage, she saw the mass of paparazzi crowded around the entrance of the tourism board office.

She called her mother on the way out of town, and then Charles, disappointment washing through her when his voice mail picked up on the second ring.

Nerves rocketed through her as she turned down her parents' street, followed quickly by relief when she saw the cul-de-sac empty of cars.

Her mother had the door open before Alice was half-way up the walk.

"Flynn," Alice whispered, scooping up the wide-eyed baby from Lynn's arms and cradling him tight to her chest.

"Alice, some of the women from my bunco group have been calling the house." Her mother's gaze was filled with worry. "They're saying—"

"I know," Alice interrupted, moving past her into the bright entry and then tugging on her arm. "Where's Dad? I need to talk to both of you."

They found her father in his study, staring at the computer screen behind his desk. He was watching a news clip from one of the most popular American gossip sites. Alice gasped as her face appeared. It showed her walking next to Charles on a city sidewalk. She was oblivious of the camera shooting footage of them, but there was no mistaking the dreamy expression on her face.

She looked like a lovesick schoolgirl.

It was mortifying to think that's how she appeared every time she looked at him. That while she was busy trying to be strong and independent, her face gave away everything she was feeling.

Her mother put a hand on her arm, as if offering support from the judgment and personal attacks aimed at her and Flynn from the tabloid report.

"Daddy."

At the sound of her voice, her father hit the mute button on the keyboard and turned in his chair.

She expected to see disappointment etched on his features, but there was only concern.

"Are you okay, Alice?"

Any other question and she could have held it together, but the reminder of how much her parents loved her in their own gentle way was too much. Tears blinded her and her mother helped her sink into the chair across from her father's desk. It was the one she'd spent hours in as a girl, reading her favorite books as he worked on syllabi and research papers.

She continued to clutch Flynn, but at his short cry she relaxed her hold on him.

"I'm fine, Dad," she lied, wiping at her cheeks. "I should have known that the story would break eventually, but I didn't want to believe it."

"So it's true?" Her mother's voice sounded dazed.

"Charles Fortune Chesterfield was your one-night stand?"

"Charles is Flynn's father," Alice said with a nod.

"It looks like more than a one-night stand from the footage they're showing of the two of you."

"I didn't tell him about the baby at first, but I realized he had a right to know his own son. Charles has been spending time with Flynn these past few weeks while he's been in town."

Lynn perched on the edge of the big desk and studied Alice. "And you, too?"

"And me, too," she whispered. "I…"

"Fell in love with him," her mother finished. "He's the man you told me you can't see in your future."

Alice pointed at the computer, where images of her still flashed, along with pictures of Charles's other girl-friends. "Look at me next to the other women he's dated. There's no comparison."

"You're right," her father agreed. "You are more beautiful than any of them."

"Not to mention you look like you have something between your ears besides air," Lynn added.

Alice sniffed, then smiled at the way her parents immediately came to her defense. "He's such a good man, much more than how he's portrayed in the press. I love being with him, love who I am when we're together. He's learning to be a great father to Flynn and I don't want it to end. But…"

Henry steepled his hands in front of him. "I don't like *but*s."

"He asked me to move to London with him."

"Oh." Her mother's shoulders slumped. "If that's what

you want, of course we'll support you. I can't imagine you and Flynn living so far away."

"I haven't heard a 'but' yet," her father said. "Is a transatlantic move what you want, Alice?"

"I don't know," she admitted quietly. "I want to be with Charles, but I'm afraid that he only asked me because of Flynn." The baby had fallen asleep in her arms and she smoothed a hand over his soft hair. "I know it sounds silly, but I want him to want *me*, not just the mother of his baby."

"That's not silly at all," Lynn told her.

"The boy would be a fool not to realize what a prize you are," her father added in his gruff voice.

"We just needed more time," Alice murmured. "Now that the story has broken—"

Lynn glanced at the computer screen and shook her head. "Turn that off, Henry. I've seen plenty from the tabloids." She looked back at Alice. "Have you talked to Charles?"

Alice shook her head in turn. "I haven't been able to reach him. He's visiting family in Horseback Hollow and I know at least one of his siblings lives out on a ranch. Maybe there isn't good cell phone reception where he is."

"So it's possible he doesn't know what you're dealing with here?"

That seemed hard to believe for a family who was so used to being tabloid fodder, but the alternative was that Charles was avoiding her. "I'm not sure. I guess so." She took a deep, shuddering breath. "The press was waiting for me outside of work today. What if they're already at my apartment? What if they come to your house?"

Her father leaned forward. "You're safe here, Alice."

"Why don't you spend the night?" her mother suggested. "You look exhausted and I don't want you to face the paparazzi on your own."

"I think I'll do that, Mom. Thank you."

"Of course, sweetie." Her mother reached for the baby as Alice stood. "You still have clothes up in your old bedroom. I'll take Flynn while you get changed, then we'll have dinner." She balanced Flynn in one arm and wrapped the other around Alice's shoulders. "We're going to get you through this."

Afraid she'd start crying again if she tried to speak, Alice simply nodded. She showered, then changed into a pair of pajama pants and a Longhorns T-shirt she'd left in her bedroom. She fed Flynn one last bottle, then put him down for the night before having a quiet meal with her mom and dad. They seemed to understand she wasn't up for more talking, and both kissed her goodnight after dinner.

She checked her phone once more before climbing into bed, but Charles still hadn't called. Instead her voice mail was full, and texts continued to pop up on the screen, with reporters and friends trying to contact her. It seemed everyone in the world wanted to speak with her, except the one person whose voice she wanted to hear.

Placing her phone in the nightstand drawer so she wouldn't have to see it continue to light up, she rested her head on the soft pillow. The sheets smelled like the detergent her mother had used for years, and the feeling of safety Alice always had in her parents' house gave her a little comfort. She turned on her side and watched Flynn through the slats of the crib set up in one corner of the room. In the glow of the night-light she could see his mouth work as he slept, unaware of the firestorm surrounding him and his mother.

She hated that he was going to grow up with reporters as part of his life. Had she compromised her vow to protect her son, by falling so hopelessly in love with Charles? What would it be like if she moved to London? Would the British press be part of her everyday life, and who would she have to protect her?

As doubts and fear careened through her mind in the silence of her childhood bedroom, her thoughts kept returning to Charles. Was he still in Horseback Hollow? Why hadn't he called her? Did the press coverage they were receiving change his plans? Had their future together been ruined before it had even begun?

Chapter Sixteen

"Hey, James Bond, do you mind taking it easy on the curves?" Charles's brother Jensen grabbed the handle of the passenger door of his oversize Chevy truck. "My truck has a lot of power but it doesn't exactly handle like an Aston Martin."

Charles saw the sign for the Horseback Hollow branch of the Redmond Flight School and Charter Service in the distance and instead of slowing down, pressed his foot harder to the gas pedal.

"You'll be no good to Alice and Flynn splattered all over the side of a rural Texas highway."

That pierced the panic swirling through Charles's mind and he forced himself to slow as he turned into the airfield. It was almost twenty-four hours since the story of Flynn's paternity had broken in the tabloids. Unfortunately, he'd been out on a ride with his brother-in-law, Quinn Drummond, when the news first hit, and had left his phone in the ranch's guest bedroom. They'd gone straight to dinner at one of the neighboring properties, and so far out of town, the reception was spotty at best.

By the time he'd gotten back to Amelia and Quinn's house, it had been almost midnight, but most of his family members were waiting for him, with various opinions on how to handle the media frenzy. The Fortunes in Horseback Hollow were somewhat insulated from the paparazzi, but Lucie had video chatted in from Austin, where an apparent media circus was raging.

He'd listened to Alice's three voice mails, her tone more desperate in each subsequent message. But he'd waited to call her back until this morning, not wanting to wake her or Flynn so late at night. That had been a terrible mistake.

Her cell phone had gone directly to voice mail each time he called, and he'd finally resorted to tracking down her parents' home number. It had taken a fair bit of convincing before her mother believed he was actually Charles Chesterfield, and when she did, Lynn Meyers wasted no time in expressing her disappointment in how he'd left Alice to fend off the tabloid press on her own. For someone known worldwide for his charm, Charles had an abysmal track record with the Meyers women.

He explained the situation as best he could, then resorted to begging for information on how Alice was dealing with everything that had transpired. The real panic had set in when Lynn informed him that Alice was planning to leave Austin to escape the press. She wouldn't tell him where her daughter planned to go, but did let him know that Alice was mostly ignoring her phone, since it was difficult to tell calls from the press from those of her friends and coworkers.

Charles's only thought was that he had to get to Alice before she left with Flynn. He was terrified that she'd disappear before he had the chance to tell her he loved her.

Because that's what had become clear to him in the midst of the tabloid furor. He didn't care if he never attended another society party again. He loved Alice and the life he had with her. She didn't need to fit into his world. He wanted to create their own perfect life together. He'd been a fool not to realize it sooner. A fact his siblings had been more than happy to point out over and over.

Even that didn't matter.

All he cared about was finding Alice.

He slammed on the brakes and threw the truck into Park, tossing the keys to Jensen as he climbed out. Charles had insisted on driving to the small airport, as he didn't trust his buttoned-up brother to get him there on time.

Orlando Mendoza, his mother's new love interest, had offered to fly him to Austin. The trip was only about an hour by air, as opposed to the six hours it would take him to drive. Six hours he didn't have if he was going to reach Alice in time.

The reality was that he could track her down even if she left Austin before he got there. But somehow in Charles's mind, getting to her first was an essential part of proving that he deserved another chance with her and Flynn.

"Thanks for your help," he called to his brother as he darted toward the small terminal building. "I'll call when I work things out."

To his surprise, Jensen caught up with him in a few steps. "I'm going with you."

Charles shook his head but didn't stop moving. "Don't be ridiculous. I can handle this."

"Believe what you want, but if you're determined to make things right with Alice—"

"I am."

"Then you need support."

"From you?" Charles paused outside the door of the hangar.

Jensen flashed a patently big brother smile. "From all of us." He pointed through the terminal's plate glass windows. Brodie, Oliver and Amelia stood talking to Orlando, next to a shiny single-engine airplane.

"You can't be serious."

"Lucie will meet us with a car in Austin."

"You don't even know Alice," Charles argued, shaking his head.

"All the more reason for us to come along for the ride. We want to meet her before you pledge your troth and all of that business."

"My troth?"

"Do you want to argue or shall we be off?" Jensen pushed through the double doors, leaving Charles no choice but to follow.

He was both annoyed with his siblings for intruding and touched that they were willing to put their own busy lives on hold to support him. But whichever emotion won out in the end, Jensen was right about one thing. Charles didn't have time to waste arguing.

He sat next to Orlando in the cockpit, not wanting to spend the flight listening to his siblings argue over how he should handle both the press and Alice.

It was a clear day, perfect for flying, and Orlando was a careful and experienced pilot. His salt-and-pepper hair was a contrast to the burnished tan of his face, and he still had the strong build of a much younger man. Charles knew Orlando was semi-retired and appreciated him arranging this trip on such short notice.

He told him as much, talking through the headsets to express his thanks. Orlando glanced at him, gave a brief nod, then focused on landing the plane on the short runway outside Austin.

As the plane touched down, Orlando finally spoke to him. "Good luck today, Charles. Your mother is proud of you for fighting for your baby and the woman you love."

"She was the one who taught me that love is worth fighting for." He flashed a self-deprecating smile. "Too bad I was never the quickest study."

Orlando returned his grin before his gaze turned serious again. "From everything your mother has told me about Sir Simon, your father would be proud of you, too."

Emotion welled in Charles's throat as he met the older man's steady brown eyes. His mother had said almost the same thing to him, but hearing it from someone who was a father to his own brood of grown children and who would have been close to Sir Simon's age made Charles feel like he was somehow gaining his own dad's blessing.

At the very least, Sir Simon would have respected Orlando, and Charles guessed the two men might have become friends. Although no one would ever take his father's place, Charles was suddenly grateful his mother had gotten another chance at happiness.

Just as he hoped to earn his own second chance with Alice.

As promised, Lucie was waiting for them behind the

wheel of an SUV large enough to fit them all, once they exited the terminal.

"How bad is it?" Charles asked. She gave him a quick hug, while Amelia, Brodie, Oliver and Jensen climbed into the back. Orlando had offered to wait with the plane so that his siblings wouldn't have to spend more than a day away from home. Charles only hoped he'd have a reason to stay in Austin.

"Have you reached Alice yet?" Lucie slid into the passenger side as he took the wheel. Charles was simply too nervous not to be in control of the driving.

He shook his head. "I rang her again as soon as we landed, but still no answer. According to her mother, she's quite upset."

"Of course she is." Lucie stared out the front window as they turned onto the main highway from the airfield.

Amelia leaned forward from the backseat. "We've grown up with the attention and it's still upsetting when a story hits. I can only imagine how that poor girl is reacting."

As could Charles, and it made his stomach turn with worry, anger and regret. He should have been more careful when they were together. He should have kept Alice and Flynn safe.

He stepped harder on the gas, ignoring Amelia's gasp as she flew back in her seat.

"No more talking," Charles growled. "If you all want to tag along, at least do me a favor and shut the hell up."

He heard Brodie bark out a laugh. "He's sounding more American by the moment."

"You'll be the first one left on the side of the road." Charles glanced in the rearview mirror. "So I advise you to close your piehole."

To Charles's amazement, that final bit of slang did the trick, and his siblings were quiet for the rest of the drive.

Alice was not surprised to hear the doorbell ring as she zipped shut her suitcase. Although most of the paparazzi had been waiting on the street in front of her building, a few had managed to sneak into the place when other residents entered. After opening her door to a microphone and camera shoved in her face, Alice had quickly learned to ignore the ringing.

She'd returned to her apartment from her parents' house early this morning under the cover of darkness. Flynn had dozed in his car seat, and Alice had sneaked into the back of her building without incident. But she hated sneaking through her own life, with the constant fear of being ambushed by the press.

The uproar over the discovery that Charles was the father of her baby would eventually die down, but their lives would never again be anonymous. There would always be an interest in Flynn. How did the Fortune family deal with that kind of scrutiny on a daily basis?

She wondered if the tabloid news had finally reached Charles in Horseback Hollow, and wished she could hear his voice. Maybe he'd called her by now, but Alice had been so frustrated with the texts and calls she continued to receive that she'd chucked her cell phone out the car window on her way home this morning. It had been impulsive and foolish, but she'd barely slept last night and wasn't thinking clearly.

The insistent knocking continued, and Flynn gave a sharp cry from his crib. Alice lifted him up, cradling him against her as she stepped into the family room and stared at the door. She'd made plans to visit an aunt who lived outside Dallas, but how was she going to leave with reporters at her door?

"Are you in there, Alice?" A crisp British voice clipped out the words. "Answer the door, love."

Her heart seemed to stop beating in her chest, and at the same time, relief washed through her. Charles would know how to handle the paparazzi. Charles would make the hell of the last twenty-four hours fade away.

Relief was followed quickly by a dizzying anger at the situation and a lingering disappointment in her handsome British playboy for not rescuing her sooner.

No.

Not rescuing.

Alice was not a woman who needed rescuing, no matter how much she'd wanted it.

Hadn't motherhood taught her she could stand on her own two feet? She was strong enough to fight for herself and her son. The question was, could she be strong enough to prove to Charles that *she* was worth fighting for?

She opened the door, planning to tell him everything she was thinking, but stopped short at the sight that greeted her. Charles wasn't alone. Two women and three men whom Alice immediately recognized as his five siblings flanked him on either side.

So much for the paparazzi. Alice was under siege by the British Fortunes.

All those aristocratic eyes staring at her were enough to make the thoughts in her head scatter.

"Alice, thank God you're still here." Charles's words had her attention snapping back to him.

"I'm actually on my way out," she said, proud that her voice remained steady despite the emotions swirling through her chest. "Flynn and I are going to visit my extended family until the worst of the attention blows over."

"You can't leave," he answered immediately, something close to panic flashing in his blue eyes.

"Why?"

One of the women, a tall, hazel-eyed beauty, leaned forward. Alice recognized her as Lucie, Charles's younger sister, who was most recently the focus of a tabloid storm centering on her secret marriage to Austin native Chase Parker. "Well, unless you have an invisibility cloak tucked away somewhere, there's a media circus on the sidewalk downstairs," she said.

Alice straightened her shoulders. "I won't let the paparazzi hold me prisoner in my own home." Even though that's exactly how she'd felt the past day.

"She's got mettle," one of the men commented, nudging Charles in the arm. "I like her already."

"It's obvious you don't deserve her," the taller man on Charles's other side muttered. "So you'd better make this good."

"Make what good?" Alice asked, a hysterical giggle rising in her throat as her gaze darted between the various Fortunes. It really was too much to have them all crowded in the hallway staring at her. She managed to tamp down both the laughter and panic, holding on to her baby like he was her anchor in a fierce storm.

"I'm not making anything good," Charles snapped.

"Clearly," the second sister, Amelia, murmured, and reached out to run a finger across Flynn's soft cheek. "He's a beautiful boy."

"Thank you."

"Charles said Flynn gives you some trouble sleeping." Amelia offered a gentle smile. "Clementine was the same way and I often wondered—"

"I'm wondering if the rest of you will be quiet," Charles practically growled, shooting angry glares at his brothers and sisters, "so that Alice and I can have a conversation."

Immediately, Amelia stopped speaking, and along with the rest of the Fortunes, looked expectantly at Charles.

"You can't leave," he repeated in a ragged whisper. "You're going to London with me. I can take care of you there. You and Flynn."

She gave a small shake of her head. "I never agreed to that, Charles. I told you I'd think about it but—"

"You have to, Alice. What's happened here proves it. You need me."

She swallowed. "I need you?"

He looked baffled that she would question him. "Flynn needs me."

At that moment, the baby let out a small cry. Alice looked between her baby and Charles.

"Let me," Amelia offered, holding out her arms. "I'll take care of him."

"Flynn is staying with me. I'm his mother." Alice wrapped her arms around the baby and stepped back into the apartment. She wasn't handing over her baby to anyone, no matter how well-meaning Charles's sister appeared.

The truth was, the Fortunes were better equipped to care for the baby, with all the demands the press would make. They were a strong family with plenty of resources to ensure that Flynn would be protected. But Alice loved Charles, and she knew it would be too difficult to be a part of his life and not have her feelings returned. Despite the valid reasons he'd given why they should be together, never once had he mentioned love.

She took a deep breath, looked him in the eye and whispered, "No."

Charles felt his chest constrict as Alice uttered that one syllable. He could hear the collective sigh from his siblings.

"You'll be a wonderful father," Alice told him, tears shining in her eyes. "And I want you to continue to spend time with Flynn, of course. But I need more."

More. How could he give her more when he was ready to offer everything he had? Everything he was.

The only answer was that *he* wasn't enough.

He started to back away, to give her the space she obviously wanted, when Lucie elbowed him hard in the ribs. "You've told her, right?"

Charles glanced at his sister. "Told her what?"

Jensen flicked him on the side of the head. "That you love her, you dunce."

Charles smacked away his brother's hand. "Stop. Beating. On. Me." He turned and threw each of his siblings a pointed glare that they seemed happy to return. "She knows I love her," he shouted.

"You love me?"

He whirled to face Alice again. "I asked you to move to another country with me. Why else would I make that offer?"

"To take care of Flynn," she answered immediately.

He felt a poke at his back. "Tell her," Lucie chided.

Of course he loved Alice. How could he not? But he suddenly realized he'd never said the words out loud.

He'd never said those three words to anyone. Maybe to his mother when he was a boy, but never as a man would say them to a woman. Not to any of the girls he'd dated. Not either of the times he'd been engaged.

Alice had already told him no. His gut told him to cut his losses and turn around before he made a bigger ass out of himself, and with the additional humiliation of his brothers and sisters to bear witness.

But another voice—one that sounded suspiciously like his father's—reminded him that he'd promised to fight for the woman standing in front of him. To prove himself worthy of her. To be a man who would make his parents proud. Even if he wound up heartbroken, he had to risk everything. Alice deserved the best he had to give.

He wanted to push her into the apartment and shut the door on his siblings. To gain a bit of privacy. But no. This had to be done here and now. No more hiding.

"I love you," he said, and bent so he was level with her beautiful—if wary—gaze. "I think I started falling in love with you that first day on the park bench."

One corner of her mouth curved as her eyes turned watery. "Really?"

"I never really understood the concept of a North Star until I met you, Alice. You are my guide in the night when I can't see anything else. You're the person who inspires me to make better choices in my life. You've shown me that I have more potential than I ever thought possible." He shot another glare over his shoulder to where his siblings stood huddled against the far wall of the corridor. "That there is more to me than anyone believed."

"You're already that person, Charles," she said softly, and his heart expanded even more.

"Only with you." He leaned in and brushed a soft kiss across her lips. "I want to take care of you, but not because you can't take care of yourself. My father taught me that one of the highest expressions of love is to take care of the people who mean the world to you. I also need you, rather desperately, I'm afraid, to care for me. To be patient, because I'm liable to make mistakes at every step."

He heard one of his brothers cough and mutter something that sounded like "not good." He shook off the distraction and focused on Alice.

"But I'll work hard to fix every one. To make you happy. To be the man you and Flynn deserve. Please give me that chance."

"What exactly are you asking, Charles?" Emotion danced in her eyes. Love for him. Devotion. Patience. It made all his fears and doubts fade away.

An image of Kate Fortune popped into his mind. He reached into his pocket for the velvet pouch that held the ring she'd given him. He'd brought it to Horseback Hollow to show his mother, and still carried it.

Without hesitation he dropped to one knee and pulled out the delicate gold band.

He heard a gasp, then a rather loud sniff behind him. Lucie, no doubt. He ignored it, continuing to stare into Alice's wide hazel eyes.

"Alice Meyers, would you do me the great honor of becoming my wife?"

"Yes," she whispered, and adjusted Flynn so that Charles could slip the ring onto her left hand. "I love you, Charles. So very much."

"Want me to take the baby so you can kiss her properly?" Jensen offered with a brotherly nudge.

"I can kiss both of them perfectly well with no help from you," Charles muttered, then folded both Alice and Flynn into his embrace. The baby laughed as Charles kissed Alice, Flynn's chubby fingers poking at each of his parents' cheeks.

His siblings let out a rousing cheer.

"Team Fortune Chesterfield," Alice said against his mouth.

"Team Us," he answered, and kissed her again. This was his future…his family. Charles intended to hold on to Alice and Flynn with every piece of his heart.

Epilogue

"Are you nervous?" Alice asked as she watched Charles take another deep breath.

They stood on the sidewalk in front of her parents' house three days after Charles had declared his love for her. In that time, the media circus that surrounded them had begun to fade, spurred by Charles's very public declaration of love for her and the announcement of their engagement.

His sisters, Lucie and Amelia, had coached Alice on how to handle the tabloid press when she did encounter them. Knowing she had the support of the Fortune family made Alice feel far more confident in her ability to cope with the public aspect of Charles's life. But right now her handsome Brit was the one who looked distinctly uncomfortable.

He balanced Flynn's infant carrier in one arm and ran

his free hand through his hair. "Of course I'm nervous. I'm about to be introduced to your parents."

She laced her fingers with his and led him up the paved walk. "You've met heads of state, Fortune 500 CEOs, celebrities from all parts of the world. My mom and dad are an ordinary couple from the suburbs of Austin." She shook her head. "Why would they make you nervous?"

He stopped, tugged on her hand until she turned to him. "Because they're important to you, Alice. They love you and I love you, so it would help if they at least liked me." He made a face. "Our courtship didn't follow the prescribed timeline. Meeting your parents after we've had a baby together and gotten engaged takes the phrase 'putting the cart before the horse' to a whole new level."

Alice laughed. She couldn't help it. Charles looked almost comically stricken. Then she brushed a light kiss over his lips. "They want me to be happy," she whispered into his mouth. "You make me happy."

She felt a little of his tension ease as he rested his forehead against hers, grounding himself in her. Since that afternoon in her apartment, Charles had become even more affectionate with her. Saying the words *I love you* out loud had freed up something in him, fragmented the last of his defenses so that now every moment they were together his touch conveyed the fact that he was well and truly hers.

It made her heart swell until it felt almost too big for her body to contain.

A throat cleared discreetly behind her and she turned to see her parents standing in the doorway. She knew Charles had nothing to worry about from Henry and Lynn Meyers.

He held out a hand as they approached. "Mr. and Mrs. Mey—"

Her mother cut him off, enveloping them both in a warm hug. "Call me Lynn," she said. "I'm so glad our Alice found you, Charles. I know you'll take good care of her."

Alice could see that her mother's faith in him bolstered Charles's own confidence. "Every moment of my life," he promised as he returned Lynn's hug. "Your daughter is a precious gift. One that I'll treasure and guard each day."

"Oh, well. That's perfect, then." Her mother took a step back, her hand pressed to her chest as if she was having trouble gathering a breath.

"The Charles Effect strikes again," Alice murmured, making him smile at their private joke.

She hugged her father, and Henry shook Charles's hand, clearly not as quickly won over as his wife but approving in his own quiet way. "I'd like to know what you Englishmen are taught about the Revolutionary War," he told Charles.

"I'd be honored to discuss that with you, sir," Charles answer, earning a small smile from Henry. At that moment Alice was certain her Fortune would fit in just fine as part of their tight-knit family.

Flynn made a small sound from his carrier, and her mother led them into the house. An hour later, Charles came into the kitchen, where Alice was helping her mother set the table for dinner.

"Everything all right?" she asked. Her father had dragged Charles off to his office soon after they'd entered, and she hoped her dad had limited the conver-

sation to details of American history and not grilled
Charles about their relationship.

"Fine," he answered, but ran a hand through his hair
at the same time. His nervous tell. "Can I speak to you
outside for a moment, Alice?"

Her mother glanced up from the vegetables she was
chopping for a salad. "We still have fifteen minutes until
the roast is ready. I can handle things in here."

Her heart suddenly beating a funny rhythm in her
chest, Alice picked up Flynn and followed Charles out
the French doors onto the covered patio of her parents'
backyard. "Is something wrong? Did my father—"

"He loves you," Charles interrupted, taking her hand
and raising her fingertips to his lips. "Both your parents
love you and Flynn so very much." He smoothed his
other hand over the baby's soft skin. "I can't imagine
taking you away from them."

"My home is with you now," she assured him, reaching into the back pocket of her jeans. "This came today."
She held up a shiny new passport. "I have one for Flynn,
too, so we can leave for London as soon as I get my
apartment packed." She shut her eyes for a moment as
emotion threatened to overtake her.

Alice meant what she said. She had no doubts about
moving to England to be with Charles, not when she was
so sure of his love. But it was still difficult to think about
leaving behind the life she'd built for herself. She was
proud of the woman she'd become in the past year, but
even more excited about creating a future with Charles.

She opened her eyes to find him looking at her with
such tenderness it made tears threaten. "I'm fine," she
whispered. "I promise."

"I have something to show you, as well." He took his

phone from his pocket and lifted the screen so she could see. "What do you think?"

It was a photograph of a gorgeous two-story brick house, not quite a mansion, but definitely larger than anywhere Alice had ever lived. There were oversize gables, a midnight blue slate roof and copper gutters that gave the home a timeless air. The photo must have been taken at the height of summer because a colorful flower garden was visible to the side of the house and a large elm tree provided shade for the inviting wrap-around porch.

"It's beautiful," Alice told Charles, covering his fingers with her own. "But I don't need an English manor to make me happy."

"That's a good thing, love." He leaned in to kiss her. "Because this house is right here in Austin."

Alice felt her jaw drop, and Charles ran a finger under her chin to tip it closed. "I may never wear a ten-gallon hat, but I'm not going to separate you and Flynn from your family. Or mine, for that matter," he added with a grin.

"Charles, thank you." Alice threw her arms around his neck and he folded her into his strong, safe embrace.

"Thank *you*," he whispered against her hair. "For making me whole. For being my home. My everything. I love you, Alice."

"I love you, Charles. With all my heart."

Flynn gave a great belly laugh as Charles held them closer, and Alice knew she had found her home.

* * * * *

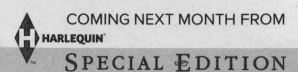
Available April 19, 2016

#2473 FORTUNE'S PRINCE CHARMING
The Fortunes of Texas: All Fortune's Children
by Nancy Robards Thompson

Daddy's girl Zoe Robinson is unsure as to the claims that her father is a secret Fortune. But she's positive about her feelings for sexy Joaquin Mendoza. Still, can Joaquin, who doesn't believe in happily-ever-afters, find love with his Cinderella?

#2474 JAMES BRAVO'S SHOTGUN BRIDE
The Bravos of Justice Creek
by Christine Rimmer

Addie Kenwright is pregnant. And her dear old grandpa gets out his shotgun to make James Bravo do the right thing. James is not the baby's daddy, but he really wants a chance with Addie...

#2475 THE DETECTIVE'S 8 LB, 10 OZ SURPRISE
Hurley's Homestyle Kitchen
by Meg Maxwell

When Nick Slater finds an abandoned baby boy on his desk, the detective is taken aback—he's not ready to be a dad! So what should he do when his ex, Georgia Hurley, shows up pregnant? This journey to fatherhood is going to be quite the family affair...

#2476 HER RUGGED RANCHER
Men of the West
by Stella Bagwell

Ranch foreman Noah Crawford is afraid of opening his heart to love. So he wants to run for the hills when his boss's beautiful sister comes calling. But Bella Sundell has no intentions of letting him go...not when he could be the man of her dreams!

#2477 DO YOU TAKE THIS DADDY?
Paradise Animal Clinic
by Katie Meyer

Jilted by a bride he never wanted, Noah James's failed honeymoon turns into a second chance at love with lovely Mollie Post. But when he discovers he's a daddy, can Noah convince Mollie their summer fling could be forever?

#2478 THE BACHELOR'S LITTLE BONUS
Proposals & Promises
by Gina Wilkins

When single and pregnant Stevie McLane confides her baby secret in her friend Cole, she never imagines that he'd propose! This marriage of convenience brings the free spirit and the widower together for the love of a lifetime.

Joaquin nodded. "It was interesting. I saw a side of your father I'd never seen before. I have acquired a brand-new appreciation for him."

"That makes me so happy. You don't even know. I wish everyone could see him the way you do."

"Thanks for having him invite me."

Zoe held up her hand. "Actually, all I did was ask him if you were coming tonight, and he's the one who decided to invite you. He really likes you, Joaquin. And so do I."

He was silent for a moment, just looking at her in a way that she couldn't read. For a second, she was afraid he was going to friend-zone her again.

"I like you, too, Zoe. You know what I like most about you?"

She shook her head.

"You always see the best in everyone, even in me. I know I haven't been the easiest person to get to know."

Zoe laughed. Even if he was hard to get to know, Joaquin obviously had no idea what a great guy he was.

"I wish I could claim that as a heroic quality," she said. "But it's not hard to see the good in you. I mean, good grief, half the women in the office are in love with you."

He made a face that said he didn't believe her.

"But I don't want to share you."

He answered her by lowering his head and covering her mouth with his. It was a kiss that she felt all the way down to her curled toes.

When they finally came up for air, he said, "In case you're wondering, I just made a move on you."

Don't miss
FORTUNE'S PRINCE CHARMING
by Nancy Robards Thompson,
available May 2016 wherever
Harlequin® Special Edition books and ebooks are sold.

www.Harlequin.com

HARLEQUIN®

A *Romance* FOR EVERY MOOD™

JUST CAN'T GET ENOUGH?

Join our social communities
and talk to us online.

You will have access to the latest
news on upcoming titles and special
promotions, but most importantly,
you can talk to other fans about your
favorite Harlequin reads.

Harlequin.com/Community

f Facebook.com/HarlequinBooks

🐦 Twitter.com/HarlequinBooks

📌 Pinterest.com/HarlequinBooks

THE WORLD IS BETTER WITH

Romance

Harlequin has everything from contemporary, passionate and heartwarming to suspenseful and inspirational stories.

Whatever your mood, we have a romance just for you!